It's All About the Song:
Joni's Songbook

Also by Barbara Light Lacy

THE GINA AND JONI BOOKS

It's Not About Love: Joni's Journal
—the first Gina and Joni story, set in
Tempe, Arizona, fall of 1972

THE AUSTINTACIOUS QUARTET

Set in 1968 Austin, Texas, written by
l.k. siga and Barbara Light Lacy

19th and University: A Tale of 1968 Austin

*Rebel Yell: June, July and August of 1968.
West, South and Lost*

Maya Karma: Journeys of Personal Discovery

Austintacious: Crowded House, Fall Semester 1968

BIOGRAPHIES

*How Suite It Is:
The Story of Robert E. Woolley and the All-Suite Hotel*

DOGUMENTARIES
(children's books told through the eyes of a dog)

Gunner's Vicarious Adventures on the Arizona Trail

Aria Finds Her Forever Family: A Min Pin Rescue Story

*The Story of Meli (Rhymes with Belly):
A Pomeranian Dogumentary*

Palusa, the Bilingual Pup: A Shih Tzu-Poodle Dogumentary

*How Max and Tootsie Became Friends:
A Big Brown Dog and a Small Yorkie Dogumentary*

*The Story of Zookie—The Dog Who Couldn't Smile:
A "Mutt" Dogumentary*

It's All About the Song:

— Joni's Songbook

Barbara Light Lacy

Golightly Publishing

Published by Golightly Publishing, Dallas, Texas
GolightlyInfo@aol.com

It's All About the Song: Joni's Songbook

ISBN 979-8-9912775-2-5 (paperback)
ISBN 979-8-9912775-3-2 (eBook)

First edition 2025

Editing by Diane Rush
Publication managed by Manon Wogahn for AuthorImprints.com
Layout and design by Kerri Esten for AuthorImprints.com

For Miss Pam,
always my forever muse.

AUTHOR'S NOTE

THIS BOOK HAS SEVERAL REFERENCES to "white crosses." For those of you who weren't around in the 1970s, white cross pills were a popular drug then. They were small white pills with a cross stamped on them. They were sold as amphetamines. White cross pills were primarily used for their stimulating effects, promoting wakefulness, increased energy levels, and enhanced focus.

Also, the dice game Horses, as played at The Hut, was commonly known as Horse.

"Pop-tops" on beer cans are also mentioned. Jimmy Buffett sings about them in one of his songs. The openings on aluminum cans used to come completely off the cans, unlike today when they stay with the can.

This book contains references to suicide.
Should you or a family member or friend
be in a crisis mode or find yourself thinking
about suicide or exhibiting suicidal tendencies,
you can reach help by
texting HOME to 741741, the Crisis Text Line,
or by calling 988, the Suicide and Crisis Lifeline,
which is staffed 24/7,
or visit their website at 988lifeline.org.

THE ROAD

Sometimes people don't know what they're looking for
And sometimes they're just looking at a wall
Sometimes they don't know when they find it
And sometimes they know nothing at all

Stop spinning your wheels
Kick up your heels
It's not very hard
To choose your boulevard

So keep your eyes wide open, keep your hands on the wheel
If the signal isn't working just go with what you feel
Because the road will take you where you need to go
Because the road will show you what you need to know
Because the road is alive and the road is real

—Joni's Songbook

Part One

JANUARY 1973

You can't take the J out of Joni
And you can't take the music out of me
And you can't take the moments
When I am happy
And you can't take away that I am free

—Joni's Songbook

CHAPTER 1

Monday, January 1. The US resumed airstrikes across South Vietnam and North Vietnam after a thirty-six-hour New Year ceasefire. Vietcong, South Vietnamese military men, and three civilians were killed. Dr. John Money of Johns Hopkins University testified in criminal court in Manhattan that people would be less likely to get divorces if they included films like *Deep Throat* in their sex education.

· ·

"IT'S THE YEAR OF THE ox, Joni. Do you know how big an ox's balls are? Do you think that means that all our men will have oxen-sized dicks this year?" Gina asked, reclining, legs askew on the sofa while holding the January issue of *Cosmopolitan* magazine in front of her chest.

"Only you would connect the year of the ox with dicks, Gina," Joni said, handing Gina a cup of coffee just as Gina liked—instant Kava, acid neutralized, which made

Gina think it was healthier. Cream and sugar added, but Joni knew better than to say anything about the extra calories.

"Why what do you mean, sweet Joni? You've been talking about watching balls fly since IBM invented the Selectric typewriter."

Joni laughed. "Yeah, well, you may be right," she said, then stopped to reflect on the year gone by.

"It was great to move in with you last fall, Gina. We had some great adventures, didn't we?"

"Yep, but you almost had us done in by the hit man in a drug deal gone wrong, and that one we didn't even know about."

"Can you let that alone?" Joni pleaded. "You're right, we didn't even know what was going on and people thought we did."

"Okay, fine. Chapter read and ended, and book closed. But I gotta admit that Jimmy Dick was a welcome addition to my stable of men."

"Yup," Joni agreed. "His mother sure did know what to give him for a middle name!"

Gina smiled, her dimples showing, then drank the last of her coffee. "Get me a mimosa, Joni. We have to start this year out right. Oh, and did you know that the first person to walk across our threshold will influence our entire year?"

"Gina, you have so many superstitions I can't remember all of them. I couldn't move the broom up here from the first-floor apartment because it would bring up bad luck, I can't sew on Sundays because I'll cry on Mondays, I can't have a hat on the bed or we'll have more bad luck, and I have to throw salt over both shoulders every time I spill some."

"Yes, true, but you spill things all the time, and even though other people only have to throw salt over one shoulder, you need the extra protection of both shoulders."

Joni couldn't argue about that one. She was a total klutz.

"Nonetheless," Gina continued, "ideally we should have a dark-headed, tall, good-looking man be the first one to cross our threshold, and even better if he is bringing some salt or bread."

"Gina, are you crazy? Like who brings us salt or bread. You sound like the Bible."

"With my mother dragging me to the Baptist Church and my father taking me to the Methodist one, I can practically quote the entire thing. We need salt so we can 'radiate with flavor.' Matthew. But trust me on this one, Joni. If a red-headed man or a blond man enters first, we are going to have bad luck all year. And if it's a woman, well, my mama said just get out your gun and shoot her. She'd bring us disaster."

"We don't have a gun, Gina."

Just then the girls heard the familiar *err-rr-rr-rr-rr* from the courtyard downstairs in their apartment complex. The girls lived on the second floor at the Windbell and kept their windows open most of the time when it wasn't too hot or cold. They also kept their door open most of the time, living in Tempe, Arizona, where the temperatures were mild, but today the front door was closed. January had set out to be a cold one, and besides, Gina was worried about the first person to cross the threshold and had even locked the front door, a rare occurrence at their apartment.

"Gina, that's Rudy. He always crows in the morning when he's happy."

"He must've gotten laid last night. I guess Martha was over."

"Yeah, he loves her but he sure spends a lot of time up here with me."

"Joni, this is the seventies. We are the sexual revolution. No one owns anyone."

The 1970s picked up where the 1960s left off. The nation's first Earth Day was in April, 1970, and the Environmental Protection Agency was formed later in 1970. 1970 saw the publication of *Our Bodies, Ourselves* and 1972 the illustrated book titled *The Joy of Sex*.

Joni thought about what Gina said. "I know, but it's still a little weird to me. Everyone knows everybody else. Everyone does everybody else. Everyone knows who everyone else is doing but not too many people are concerned about it..." she said, thinking about the past few months, then moving to the window and getting down on her knees. The windows in the Windbell Apartments opened from the bottom at the floor. Joni pushed up the window and called out into the courtyard.

"Rudy, oh Rudy. Do you have a moment? We need some salt. Can you bring us a cup?"

Rudy stopped crowing and thought, What in the world do these girls want with a cup of salt? but knew better than to ask. They were crazy as hoot owls and more fun than two puppies.

"Sure, hang on a minute," Rudy said, turning and going back into his apartment.

Joni turned to Gina and said, "Okay, we're getting a tall, dark-haired man to bring us a cup of salt. The fact that I asked him to do that won't matter, right?"

Gina laughed. "No, I don't think so. You are so adept at messing with the cosmic forces! Can you get me another mimosa?"

"Coming right up," Joni said, "with another one for me on the side."

"Coming? I'd sure like to do that on January first. Then I'd be doing it the entire year long."

"You do it the entire year long anyway, silly girl!"

"Yes, Joni, but this is the first day of a new year. Whatever happens today will set the table for the rest of the whole year. Our fate is at risk."

Joni laughed and headed to the kitchen to make their drinks. Just then,

THERE CAME A KNOCK AT THE DOOR

"Who is it?" Gina singsonged. There was no way the wrong person was going to come over that threshold.

"It's Rudy. Joni ordered a cup of salt." Joni went to the door, unlocked it, pulled it open, and smiled.

"Here's your salt," Rudy said, extending his right arm into the apartment, the cup of salt held tightly in it. He remained on the concrete breezeway that connected their apartment to the apartments on the other side of the courtyard.

"Oh Rudy, dear boy, please bring it to me," Gina said, singsonging again and not moving at all from her perch on the sofa.

Rudy shrugged with a what-the-hey look on his face and walked into the apartment.

"Woo-hoo," Gina said. "A tall, dark-haired man bearing the gift of salt—our first visitor after midnight and he's over the threshold. I can feel this year gearing up to be a good one."

Rudy looked at Joni, who laughed and said, "One of Gina's superstitions—if Andi had come over here, we would have had to shoot her. No way could a girl walk over the threshold first or disaster would have befallen us."

"But you don't have a gun," Rudy said.

"Right on, fella, but Gina would have figured out something. Thanks so much for the salt. We'll return the cup to you later." She walked back to the kitchen with the salt, then turned to face Rudy. "Unless you want to stay and have a mimosa with us."

"Sounds good, but a friend of mine crashed down-stairs last night and I need to get his ass up and moving. The football games start shortly."

"Well, Rudy," Gina said, "why don't you just go get him and we'll make mimosas for both of you guys. Scurry, Joni, get thyself into the kitchen, you wench!" Then, "Uh, what color hair does he have?"

"Dark, like mine, dear Gina. Does that work for you?"

"Perfect. I think it is really only the first man to cross the threshold, but you can't be too sure, and two are almost always better than one."

Rudy went downstairs. Joni pulled more glasses from the cabinet. Gina picked up the *Cosmopolitan* again while she waited for her mimosa.

"Listen to this, Joni. It says here that the mudpack has been rediscovered. A company named Arizona Natural Resources makes Down-to-Earth, a face mask made from mud. Says it's the same reddish-brown mud that Indian women liked for its magical properties. We gotta get some of that."

"Why don't we just go dig some up, Gina?"

"How would we ever know where to go to dig? We might end up with the wrong mud and then what? No magical properties and we could risk some bad mojo."

"Gina, you are just too funny!"

Gina was turning to the article on how sex can make you slim when Rudy and his friend, wearing a T-shirt that said "Let Us Tickle Your Fancy," walked through the door. Gina thought that was a very good sign.

"Hi girls," Rudy said. "This is Wheeler. I met him in one of my classes at the university a couple of years ago and now he's a pool hustler. Wheeler, this is Gina"—he pointed to the sofa—"and over there is Joni." He then pointed to the kitchen where Joni was just picking up two freshly made mimosas and carrying them to the boys.

Joni went back to the kitchen and got Gina's glass and the plastic tumbler that held her mimosa.

The four lifted their glasses in a toast to the new year.

"Hmm, great mimosa," Wheeler said, wondering why Joni's mimosa was in a plastic tumbler instead of a glass, but saying nothing. "I heard that this was the place to be to have fun."

"You got that right, young man." Gina grinned, showing her dimples. "Are you really a pool hustler? Joni and I play pool. We aren't very good at it but we do pretty well hustling drinks that way."

"Yeah, I play pool a lot and have gotten good over the years, but it's more of a hobby. I'm a long-haul truck driver for Phil Fancy's Fruits & Vegetables. Tempe is my home base but I'm gone weeks at a time hauling the produce across the country. Once I took forty-five thousand pounds of green tomatoes from Florida to Los Angeles and I had to get them there before they turned red. It was quite the adventure," Wheeler said, raising his eyebrows and blushing slightly.

"I can see that," Gina said, raising her own eyebrows and wondering how to get into his action.

"Aha," Joni said. "Is that what your T-shirt is about?"

Wheeler laughed. "Yup, Phil thought that was a funny line. Most of the shirts have tomatoes and oranges on them, but I prefer the ones with just our tagline. Gets the girls every time."

"Ick, tomatoes," Gina said. "Don't you know they hold all the poison of the earth. No tomato will ever cross these lips."

Joni, laughing out loud, said, "Right, but you suck down ketchup like it was Budweiser."

"That's quite a different story, Joni. I'm certain the vinegar in ketchup does away with the poison."

Joni wasn't about to argue with Gina. Everyone just laughed and took another swallow of their mimosa.

"We're going to The Hut later this afternoon. You two boys want to join us and maybe pick up a game of pool? There's no specials on Monday, but it *is* the first day of the year. What you do matters for the next three hundred sixty-four days."

"Thanks for the offer, Gina, but we're gonna watch football all day today with a bunch of the guys downstairs. You girls are always welcome, but I think it's more of a locker-room style of event," Rudy said. "We're all looking forward to the Rose Bowl, Ohio State against the number one rated team, Southern California, the USC Trojans. Gonna be a real nail-biter."

"Better than a ball-biter," Joni said.

"Joni's fixated on balls today," Gina said, thinking that it was every day Joni was fixated on balls. "Just ignore her." Everyone laughed again.

"Okay, girls," Rudy said. "We're going downstairs now. Thanks for the mimosas."

"Catch you on the flip-flop," Wheeler said. The girls looked at him quizzically. "It's trucker talk and it means when I get back this way."

It was early afternoon. The Windbell, at 1300 W. Broadway and Priest, was a new apartment complex catering to students at the college and also to the singles crowd. Gina had moved into a one-bedroom apartment there last fall. Joni, on her way back to Texas from Utah, stopped in to visit Gina and decided to stay. After all, four men to every woman in Tempe was enticing. A month later, the girls moved upstairs to a two-bedroom apartment, which made it much easier to entertain the boys than when Joni had to spread her sleeping bag out on the floor in the living room downstairs if she brought home a man. Joni had been sleeping in the walk-in closet in the hallway of Gina's apartment.

The sun was bright and had warmed up the air. Joni opened the door to the apartment to let the other tenants know the girls were ready for anything. Almost everyone in their building at the Windbell had enjoyed a party of one kind or another at the girls' apartment over the past few months. An open door was an easy invitation.

Gina remained spread out on the sofa skimming *Cosmopolitan* and reading to Joni from time to time. Joni had turned on KDKB, the free-form radio station that always tripped her trigger. KDKB played album rock interspersed with hit singles. Legend had it that the station played ocean wave recordings for several days before it went live. "Me and Mrs. Jones" by Billy Paul was playing as Joni turned up the volume.

"Joni, listen to this. The article is called 'Can Adultery Save Your Marriage?' Most people say yes, and some affairs have been going on for years."

"We're not married, Gina."

"Well, it will be a good thing to know if we ever are." Gina could make sense of anything. "Should we start getting ready to go to The Hut?"

"I'm hungry," Joni said, scrunching up her eyes and tightening her lips, an expression she had seen on Gina's face more than once.

"Quit whining, Joni. We'll stop by the Dash Inn first and have a hamburger. Maybe Richard will be there and you can start your year with a Mexican cook."

"Maybe, but then I'd have to sleep with non-circumcised men all year long, and I'd prefer a variety."

"Thanks again for sharing him with me last year. I think that was a first for both of us, a non-circumcised man." Gina and Joni had an unwritten rule—no messing around with the other person's man unless it was agreed upon by both of the girls. Joni had slept with Richard the Mexican cook first but wanted to share the experience of sex with an uncircumcised man with Gina.

"Yup," Joni said. "We've shared some good times, we've been through some strange times, and we even remember some of them! I can't wait to see what happens this year."

"Me either, but I suggest you shouldn't be doing any more drug dealers."

"Who knew, Gina, who knew?"

Both girls were quiet then, Gina back to reading, Joni wondering what ever did happen to Pilot after she dropped him off at the ramp to the freeway that night last month. Rumors after his disappearance included Pilot being killed in the desert, Pilot being a government agent, and Pilot just being one stupid drug dealer. It had been a good time, but Joni was glad it was over. There were enough men in Tempe for her to play with, so she didn't need just one to entertain her. Pilot had made it sound like he wanted to move in. And then there was the hit man.

"Uh, and Gina—"

Gina looked up at Joni with a scowl for interrupting her reading.

"We've already met one new guy this year, so that's what we will be doing all year long, according to your theory."

"Works for me," Gina said, going back to her magazine. "And check this out—we can get four books for a dollar if we join the Book-of-the-Month Club. Of course we need to buy four more later, but look at these titles." She pointed to the page. "*Everything You Always Wanted to Know About Sex. The New York Times Cook Book.* You know how I love to read cookbooks." Gina looked at Joni, laughing. "Maybe you should read more of mine—you are such a bad cook, Joni."

"Yeah, well, I try. It's not my fault you didn't like lentils."

Gina turned up her nose and scrunched her face, remembering when Joni first arrived in Tempe and offered to cook with whatever was in the house and in Joni's truck. Who knew that Joni traveled with lentils? Who knew anyone who traveled with lentils?

"Joni," said Gina, "say not that word one more time in this house. Anyway, get Rod McKuen's poetry and you get three books that count only as one. And, *Bury My Heart at Wounded Knee.* I'm going for it."

"Very cool. I love Rod McKuen's poetry. But why *Bury My Heart at Wounded Knee*?"

"Ah, you forget. I have enough Indian blood in me to get a number. I just chose not to do it. And I'm lucky that my ancestors were not part of the ones who were herded onto places where they died, although I have heard tales of their suffering. I'm betting this book is powerful."

"Can't wait. Let's drop the postcard into the mail today."

"Joni, no mail today. It's New Year's Day."

"Yeah, well... Okay, I'll go clean up the kitchen instead. And there's no room in the cabinets to put anything."

"Of course not. I planned it that way. The larders *must* be full on New Year's Day so we are assured prosperity all year long. I shopped all last week to be sure we'd be okay."

"What else for today, Gina?" Joni knew Gina would have more superstitions they had to adhere to.

"Money. Our wallets must be full."

"Oh that's going to be easy. I have a stash of change in my closet I can turn into bills and stuff into my wallet. Any 'rules' about how long it has to stay there? I'd like to buy a pitcher at The Hut."

"Don't be flip, Joni. These are all important New Year's Day items. And no, the money doesn't have to stay there any set amount of time. It just has to be there. Like the cabinets, we could eat it all today if we liked."

"I'd rather have a hamburger at the Dash Inn," Joni said, pouting.

"You're on. Let's get dressed, eat a burger, and then hit The Hut. Who knows what's going on there today."

"As you said long ago, dear Gina, all adventures start at The Hut. I'm up for anything." She jumped up, went to her bedroom, and opened her closet. "What am I going to wear, Gina?" she called into the living room.

"Does it really matter? All your clothes look alike anyway."

Gina went into her bedroom and put on her wheat jeans with a black top, a turquoise necklace around her neck, silver bracelets on her arms. Joni had on blue jeans and a shirt her mother had made her, paisley with a yoke and gathered material Joni was sure made her boobs look bigger. Gypsy hoop earrings and one of Gina's turquoise rings.

"I'll drive," Gina said. "I think we'll have to keep the top up on Pucci with this cool weather though." Gina had named her orange convertible Fiat Spider "Pucci" because Marilyn Monroe wore the designer Pucci's clothing.

"Works for me. I'm up for riding today. Riding anything..."

"Joni, is your mind always on taking off your pants?"

"Pretty much!" Both of them laughed.

Gina opened the door to her orange Fiat Spider at the same time that Joni opened the door on the passenger side. They jumped in and headed to the Dash Inn on Apache Boulevard. Pulling out of the parking lot of the Windbell, Gina turned left onto Broadway and headed east up to Mill Avenue.

"Gina, don't forget I need to change all these coins for bills so I can have a full wallet today."

"Joni, sometimes you are just one big hassle!" Gina smiled at her best friend and pulled into the first Circle K they saw so Joni could get dollar bills for the change she had saved in her closet. Then she drove them to the Dash Inn, and they hurried through a late lunch of hamburgers and beer.

The girls usually met at The Hut after work, but this being New Year's Day, they went midafternoon after their lunch, not knowing what to expect.

"I don't know why you think there are going to be guys there, Gina. They're all home watching football."

"Yeah, you're probably right, but maybe some of them don't like football. Or maybe they want to drink beer while they watch the game."

"On that little old black-and-white TV in the corner by the back door at The Hut? Like sure. There's usually nothing but snow on that TV."

"Okay, Joni, but you said it this morning, all adventures begin at The Hut."

"Fine," Joni said, baring her teeth and pretending indignation, which only served to cause Gina to break out laughing.

"You know, Joni, I laugh more with you than with anyone else."

"And you are the funniest person I've ever known. Also the most lucky. You always win."

"Na-na-na-na-na-na!" Gina sang as she turned off Mill Avenue onto Second Street, cruising slowly past Monti's La Casa Vieja steak house on the left just before The Hut. Then she turned left into the alleyway that ran beside the cinder block building that housed The Hut, and parked in back.

The girls walked around to the front door, pulled it open, and were immediately surprised to see the stools along the long bar on the left side of the building filled with guys shouting, "Go, go, go" and "Oh, missed that one" as the boys facing the television shouted to the set. The girls looked toward the back door and saw the reason—a new eighteen-inch Emerson color television that had taken the place of the old, smaller black-and-white one.

"Hey, Florina," Gina called to the bartender, "what's going on in the corner?"

"A boon for the bar," Florina said, smiling and walking up to the girls. "Vince picked it up for just over three hundred and fifty dollars and installed it this morning. There was a major to-do getting it to hook up with the antenna, and I was sure someone was going to fall off the roof while they tried, but they got it done. I never thought he'd pop for that, but look what happened—a full bar on football day!" Vince and his wife Bernice owned the bar and they were well known for not wanting to spend money on the place, only make money from it. "It's a total blessing."

Gina smiled and raised her eyebrows, saying, "In more ways than you know, Florina, in more ways than you know," and thinking, What a big group of guys to choose from today.

"If you two girls are finished discussing the state of the world, could we have a pitcher of beer and two glasses, *por favor*?" Joni said. Joni liked to use her Spanish, limited as it was, as often as possible with Florina, hoping for that extra pitcher of beer Florina provided for free from time to time.

Florina shrugged while smiling. "Sure, coming right up. I'll set everything at the last two unoccupied stools down by the jukebox." She knew that the girls preferred to sit at the bar rather than the two booths across the room or the room at the front where none of the regulars liked to sit. Both were too far away from the action for Gina and Joni.

The girls had just settled into the two empty stools when Florina appeared, setting the pitcher between them, a glass on either side, a bar coaster for Gina and two for Joni. Florina had watched Joni doodle on coasters for the past three months since Joni's arrival in Arizona and had thrown enough of them away with Joni's "art" on them. Fortunately, the beer distributors supplied the coasters, so it didn't matter to Vince that his bartenders threw some away. Vince also knew that the girls spent a lot of money at The Hut and were good for business because if the girls were there, the boys came in, too, so he put up with their antics.

"Hey," Gina said to Joni, "it's the Rose Bowl, the same game that Rudy and Wheeler and the boys downstairs were going to watch. They could have come along with us today."

"Yes, but then we couldn't have had our choice of men, we'd have to be with them. But it looks like all frat guys here today anyway, not my favorite."

"Not *all* frat guys," Gina said, turning her head to the right, rolling her eyes the same way for Joni to look over at the booth on the opposite wall.

"Ah, Leroy B. and Joe Ravioli. And look," Joni said excitedly, "they have their guitars."

"More than I can say for you," Gina scolded. "You've been here three months and I've never seen that old Gibson come out of its case once."

Joni looked down. "Okay, Gina. I am going to pick up my guitar this year."

"Then you'd better do it today, because what we do today we'll do all year."

Joni shrugged. It had been a while since she had played, and even longer since she had written a song. She wondered if her songs had dried up.

"Come on, Joni. It isn't the end of the world. Pick up your beer and we'll go over and sit with Leroy B. and Joe Ravioli." She got off her stool, picked up her glass and the pitcher, and kicked Joni in the ankle as she did, an extra reminder for Joni to get up.

Joni picked up her glass and both coasters, following Gina across to the booths on the other side of the pool table that sat between the booths and the bar.

"Happy New Year!" Gina said to the boys, her smile wide, her eyebrows raised. "Want some company?" she asked, using a line she had heard a hooker say in a play during college. Gina had been a drama major.

"Hey, we saw you walk in but didn't want to interfere with your conversation with Florina," Joe Ravioli said. "So good to see you. You remember my friend Leroy B. He sings with me at the Inner Ear Coffee House at the University Lutheran Church on campus."

Leroy B. looked at Gina and stood up and offered her room on his side of the booth. "Please, join us."

Gina slid in and kept her smile, although this time aiming it at Leroy B. Joni sat next to Joe Ravioli.

The quartet drank the pitcher the boys had and then the pitcher the girls brought over, chatting about who knew whom and what was what. When both pitchers were empty, Joe Ravioli rose to get another.

"Anything else you want?" he asked the group.

"Yes," Gina said loudly. "I want Joni to play a song. We noticed that you brought your guitars."

"Well, the frat guys are not going to like the music when they are watching the Rose Bowl, so why don't we go to my place? It's just down the street," Leroy B. said.

Joe Ravioli put down the empty pitchers and said, "Great idea. A jam session is better than a football game any day in my world." They all waved to Florina on their way out.

Leroy B. lived in a small apartment on Second Street but with enough room for the four people and two guitars. Joe Ravioli had two six-packs of beer in his car and brought them in. As everyone settled, the beer bottles opened. Leroy B. took out his Martin D-28 and Joe Ravioli his Martin D12-20, a twelve-string guitar, and they started jamming in the key of E, eight-bar blues. The girls listened and Joni hummed along with them, singing about love lost and found and holes in hearts. Typical, Joni thought, but the way it was with a blues song.

Joe Ravioli put down his guitar. Leroy B. handed his over to Joni, saying, "Okay, chickie, it's your turn. Gina told me you wrote songs and sang."

Joni thought, Don't freak, don't freak. Be cool. Be you. Just be you.

"Okay, I'll give it a shot. Okay if I sing one of my own songs?"

"But not 'Fungus Among Us,'" Gina said. "Do one of your other songs, maybe 'Singing the Blues in Texas.'"

Joni smiled. That one was easy. Three chords in the key of D. Joni began strumming and started with the chorus.

> *I'm singing the blues in Texas*
> *Thinkin' about you-u-u*
> *I'm singing the blues in Texas*
> *Since you said we were through*

"Hey, great song," Leroy B. said when she had finished singing all the verses.

Joe Ravioli had said nothing for a bit, then, "I had no idea you played guitar, sang, *and* wrote songs. Where have you been hiding that?"

"In her closet." Gina rolled her eyes. "I've been on her butt for the last three months to get that guitar out but oh, no, she was more interested in other things."

Joni punched Gina playfully in the arm. "Get a grip, Gina. These last three months in Tempe have been too full of fun and action to play music. Maybe this year is my time to warble." She thought that she really needed to do some picking to get the callouses back on the ends of her fingers. Leroy B.'s guitar had much stronger strings than she used, and her fingertips were barking at her.

"Warble?" said Leroy B. "You sound more like a songbird."

Joni lowered her eyelids and blushed.

"Trust me," Gina said. "Joni can sing like a songbird but she can also screech. Just watch out!"

The boys picked up the guitars again and played a few songs, then put down the guitars, emptying the last of the beer bottles. Joe Ravioli stood up, saying,

"I need to go home. Got to get to work tomorrow at the Green Ashes Crematorium. Always busy after a holiday."

"Shall I bring the marshmallows?" Gina said, smirking and showing her dimples.

"Gina, you are such a bad girl!" Joe Ravioli said. "We do *not* roast marshmallows at the Green Ashes Crematorium. You know that. The heat itself would not only disintegrate the sugar but also melt whatever you were using to hold the marshmallows. I guess you could put them in with the corpse if you wanted to add sweetness."

Joni rolled her eyes. Gina was always making bad jokes. Joe Ravioli seemed to be able to do the same.

But Gina was not listening. Leroy B. had already taken hold of Gina's hand and was pulling her to the bedroom. Joni, wondering how she would get home, said, "Joe, can you take me back to the Windbell?"

"Sure," he said. "Be glad to take you anywhere, Joni. Only a short walk down to the Quonset hut where I live and we can pick up my truck and I'll have you home in no time."

CHAPTER 2

Tuesday, January 2. The United States admits the accidental bombing of a Hanoi hospital in Vietnam. A majority of both houses of Congress voted to cut off US funds for the Vietnam War after the US prisoners of war were released. Nothing happened despite the vote of the Democrats because President Nixon and most Republicans were opposed to the cutoff of funds.

· ·

GINA GOT HOME SOMETIME IN the night, but Joni had slept through that. Not knowing if Gina was home or not, Joni jumped up and went to Gina's bedroom when she heard Gina's alarm go off. Gina, who rarely woke up to her alarm, was wrapped around her pillows and tangled in her comforter. Pushing the button on Gina's Westclox Snooze clock that would delay the alarm for another few minutes, Joni reached over and shook her friend, singing, "Good morning to you, have a wonderful day, my G-I-N, G-I-N, G-I-N-A."

"Joni, do *not* talk to me about G-I-N," Gina said, growling. "Leroy B. had a stash of gin and I may never drink again."

Joni smiled.

"Well, maybe. And besides, I have seven minutes before that clock goes off again, so go make me some coffee." Gina pulled at the comforter to get it over her head.

Joni went to the kitchen and put the water on to boil in the teapot. Gina always let the teapot boil until it whistled, but Joni usually took it from the stove just before that noise. Not today—she let it sit on the stove until the singing of the teapot and the Westclox alarm were both filling the apartment with noise.

"Wake up, Gina."

Gina got out of bed and said, "*Fine. Fine, fine, fine.*" Then, smiling at Joni, "I know you don't have to work today, so just help me get ready. And bug your temp agency to get you some work so you have enough money to pay the rent next month. We certainly don't want to move back into a one-bedroom apartment."

"You're right about that. My bed wouldn't fit into that walk-in closet I slept in when I moved here!" A woman at one temporary job mentioned that she was giving away a bed, and Joni jumped on it. For the three months before the girls moved to the two-bedroom apartment, Joni had spent most of her nights on the floor in a sleeping bag inside Gina's walk-in closet in the one-bedroom apartment.

Gina readied for work at the insurance agency. Joni got Gina the coffee, along with a breakfast of toast and cheese—a white cross on the side—and started cleaning. She hadn't gotten much done yesterday.

"When you get home tonight, you're going to be so happy because I'm cleaning this place from top to bottom."

"Really? You're even going to do my laundry?"

This hadn't been on Joni's list of things to do, but why not? Keeping Gina happy was important.

"Sure, Gina, I'll do as much of it as I can." Gina hated to do laundry and rarely picked up her clothing, preferring to pile dirty clothes in her closet and pick out what was still wearable until she couldn't get into her closet anymore. Joni had no assignment from her temp agency today so why not take care of the apartment?

Gina was dressed for work and sitting at the gateleg table in front of the window, sipping her coffee, eating her toast and cheese. She had already downed the white cross to be sure she'd have enough energy to get through the day. Joni sat at the other side of the table.

"So," Joni said. "How was the first day of the new year?"

"Silly girl. Perfect for me. I got to come into the new year with a bang. You sang a song. What could be better?"

"I'm not sure. Do you think the second day of the year also matters?"

"Sure it does. It's an extension of the first day. Let's see what happens and I'll meet you at The Hut after work."

"Cool beans. Toodle-oo," Joni said as Gina left for work.

Joni walked into Gina's bedroom and gathered up as many dirty clothes as she could carry, then walked downstairs to the laundry room in her building and shoved them into the washer. After inserting the quarters in the coin slots on the washing machine, Joni went back to the apartment to clean the kitchen. The first thing she saw was the cup full of salt. She dumped the salt into a Tupperware container, then carefully rinsed and dried Rudy's cup and thought, Hmmm, maybe Rudy is up for something. She laughed to herself . . . *up* for something . . . and smiled at the thought.

Joni walked downstairs and knocked softy on the door to Rudy's apartment, knowing that the boys may be sleeping in after all the football yesterday. Joni was surprised when Wheeler answered the door. His face turned to a smile when he saw Joni.

"Well, hello, little lady."

"Well, hello to you, too. I just came to return this cup to Rudy."

"He went over to Martha's after the games yesterday, but I'll take care of the cup for you. Thanks for bringing it back. What's happening with you today?"

"Cleaning the apartment and doing Gina's laundry. My temp agency didn't have anything for me so I'm home all day. In Texas they say 'Come on down' but I guess in this instance, I should say 'Come on up'!"

"Sounds good to me. I need to take a shower and make some calls. How about in a few hours?"

"Sure," Joni said, thinking, A day off, a tall, dark-haired man in the apartment with me on a sunny afternoon—what could be better?

Joni finished Gina's laundry, hanging up the shirts and folding the rest of the clothes, then washed all the dishes in the kitchen. She opened the door to be hospitable to Wheeler, but the unseasonably cool weather caused her to shut it again. She wondered if he was really going to show up anyway.

When all the housework was done, Joni pulled out her Gibson LG-1 guitar, set it on the sofa, then went to the kitchen and poured herself a glass of wine. She threw a coaster onto the coffee table, being careful not to knock it over—one of the table legs was not hooked on so the table only balanced on it—and set the wine down. Then with the guitar in hand, she gracefully settled onto the living room floor. It was one of the few things Joni ever did gracefully—descending to the floor with her legs crossed.

After making sure the guitar was in tune, she pulled the flat pick out of her jeans pocket. She started singing,

It's the misery of knowing I can't take you home with me
Misery that's growing 'cause I need your company
But the children and the mortgage
The neighbors and the dog
These stories that you're telling me
I know will never stop,

one of the songs she had written for a past love who neglected to mention that he was married, when

THERE CAME A KNOCK AT THE DOOR

Hoping it was Wheeler, she said, "Lock's broken, door's open."

Wheeler walked in, smiling. "Heard that music. Great song. I didn't know you played."

"I started on a ukulele that my mother got for me with S&H Green Stamps when I was fifteen and starting writing songs, then moved to a guitar, but it's been a while since I picked up my guitar here in Arizona. I got caught up in the Tempe tales last fall after I stopped to visit with Gina."

"Yeah, things get in the way sometimes, don't they? Would you let me play your guitar? I don't write songs but I play a bit."

"Sure, but everyone who has played it agrees that the action is difficult. I've had it tweaked a few times but most people still find the action to be too tight." She was surprised that a truck driver/pool hustler would play guitar.

"Not to worry, Joni. I crank up the wheels of the trailers on my trucks and pull down the doors on the back. My hands are pretty strong. Beautiful guitar, by the way," he said, taking the Gibson into his arms, sitting on the sofa, and singing a Hank Williams song.

"Wow," Joni said when he was done. "You have a wonderful voice. Great song and I appreciate you singing to me. Uh, would you like a beer?"

"Sure, thanks for asking." Joni got up off the floor and walked into the kitchen, returning with a beer for Wheeler and another glass of wine for herself. Wheeler accepted the beer and slugged it down. He stood up before Joni could sit back on the floor, pulling her toward him, then picking her up and carrying her back toward the bedrooms.

"Which one's yours?"

"The one on the left," she answered in a whisper.

It was almost five o'clock. Joni woke and realized that she had promised Gina to meet her at The Hut. She nudged Wheeler and said, "Hello, driver. I need to meet Gina at The Hut in a few. Want to join us?"

Wheeler stretched and smiled. "Thanks for the offer, but I'm heading out tonight at midnight and I can't be drinking anymore. I drive a 1970 Peterbilt with a 903 Cummins engine and a thirteen-speed transmission and it's calling to me.

"Wow, that sounds pretty impressive."

"It's one of the best and if you take care of it, it will last forever. And Joni, thanks, too, for the lovely afternoon." Wheeler smiled even wider.

Joni blushed. "Where will you be going?"

"You never know, Joni. You never know."

After Wheeler left, Joni pulled on her black turtleneck sweater and blue jeans, borrowing a silver necklace from Gina for glitz. She scooted to The Hut, parked in the back, ordered a pitcher and two glasses from Florina, and had just settled onto the stool when Gina arrived.

"Guess who I did today?" Joni said excitedly before Gina even sat down.

Gina scrunched up her face and tried to hide a smile, saying, "You mean who you did while *I* was at work? Ha. I assume Rudy, if Martha wasn't watching."

"Well," Joni drawled, picking up her glass and slowly taking a sip. "That's what I had in mind, but . . ."

"But what, Joni. Spill the beans." Gina downed her glass of beer and refilled it from the pitcher.

"Wheeler!"

"Wheeler? Bitch! I was hoping to sink my teeth into him first. But that's okay, he's yours now." The girls had long ago made a pact not to mess with each other's man, something that happened only when agreed upon, like with Billy Bob in Austin and Richard the Mexican cook here in Tempe.

"Thanks, Gina. It just happened."

"Yep. Things happen. You never know."

Joni's eyes widened. "Whoa. That's exactly what Wheeler said. 'You never know.'"

"Joni, 'You never know' is not one of the world's most profound statements."

Joni took a sip of her beer, thinking about it. "Sort of like what Michael A. always says, 'Caca pasa, chachalaca.'"

"Right, Joni, except he never told you exactly what that meant."

"Maybe next time I talk to him he will. Or maybe we'll get to hear it in person if he comes out here to visit the Green Ashes Crematorium . . . and *you* can ask him because people always tell you things." Michael A. was a silent partner in the crematorium where Joe Ravioli worked. The girls knew Michael A. from their days in Austin where Michael A. still lived. They had never mentioned that to anyone in Tempe, not even to Joe Ravioli. Michael A. was his own man, and if the circles were going to cross, it would be Michael A.'s doing.

Joe Ravioli walked up just then. "Did I hear you girls talking about the crematorium? I just got off work and after a long day with the ovens, I sure need a cold one."

"Was your day fried, roasted, or sautéed?" Gina asked, eyes squinched, head moving from side to side.

"You are *so* bad, Gina," he answered. "More like just hellaciously hot!"

"Florina, bring this boy the coldest beer in town—on us," Gina said.

Florina smiled and walked to the cooler. She knew Gina was a jokester and that Joe Ravioli always asked for a cold one when he got off work.

It was a full house at The Hut. First day at work after the holiday weekend. Too cool to walk in the park. The frat boys had a pool tournament going. The regulars were there—Craig from Colorado, Boston Jack, Max, Bobbie, Carol, Leroy B., and of course Boyer, who had always been available for Joni anytime she wanted him.

Joe Ravioli got his beer and politely excused himself to put his quarter on the pool table. A short blond guy came up to the girls, a skinny blonde girl behind him, the guy putting out his hand to shake, saying, "Hi, I'm Pete Groat, and you must be the Mill Avenue Hussies!"

Joni wasn't sure whether to take offense or not. Gina stepped up immediately and said, "You got that right, dude. Who's the scarecrow with you?" Punch and punch.

"Oh, that's Caffy. She's my friend, harmless." He turned around, giving Caffy a quarter, saying, "Go put my quarter on the pool table." She took the quarter and walked over to the pool table.

"Caffy?" said Joni. "What kind of name is that?"

Pete started laughing. "Ah, give her a break. Her mother wanted to call her Cathy, but her mother has a speech impediment and the doctor heard 'Caffy' and wrote that on the birth certificate. She's just lived with it since then. You gotta admit, it's definitely distinctive."

Gina and Joni were laughing. "Okay," Gina said. "We'll just take her as 'Caffy' and try not to laugh. Mr. Pete Groat."

"Peter Aloysius Groat to you, if you don't mind." He bowed from the waist and smiled. "But really, just call me Pete."

"Okay, Pete. How come we never met you before?" Gina asked. "We're regulars here, as you apparently know."

"I've been working the night shift for about six months now, sometimes out of town, so by the time you get here after your work, I'm already at my job. I repair locks on jail cells."

The girls just looked at each other, thinking, What in the world?

But Pete Groat continued. "Just got turned around the first of the year so now I work days, and I'm happy for it. I see you know Joe Ravioli. He's mentioned you to me many times."

"Yep, one of our best friends. Lives down the street in one of the Quonset huts," Joni said.

"Yeah, I know. I live over at Peckerwood."

"*Peckerwood?*" Gina shouted, although no one noticed over the noise in the bar.

"It's down there on First Street sort of near the Quonset huts on the other side of the street. A big house with six of us or so and a little house made out of river rock that Calvin lives in. Shotgun Calvin, we call him—he's a nine-and-one-half-finger hillbilly and he keeps us laughin'. Only ninety bucks a month that we all split, so who can complain."

"All men, I presume," Gina said politely, thinking, Hmmm, this could be fun.

"I don't think a girl could live there. The planes go over it on the way to Sky Harbor Airport, and you have to shut up until they pass. They're pretty close to the ground at that point and sometimes the walls shake. Of course not in the rock house, but in the main house."

"Sounds delightful," Gina said, this time turning up her nose.

Joni thought, Hmmm, if I was making noise while doing the deed, no one could hear... "Well, Pete, we look forward to seeing you around." The girls smiled as Caffy informed Pete it was his turn at the pool table.

Turning back to the girls, Pete said, "Hey, we're having a party at Peckerwood on Friday night. Why don't you hussies join us? Just drive down First Street and you'll see it, or hear it!" He smiled. "There's a fence around the compound and an old Hodaka motorcycle leaning up against it. Has only one peg. I can tell you stories of me trying to ride that hog with only one peg... Ah, but not now," he added as Caffy pulled on his arm and dragged him to the pool table.

"Caffy," Gina said to Joni. "What a name. It's going to be hard for me to handle that without laughing if I actually have to talk to her."

"You can't laugh, Gina," Joni said. "Because if you do, I'll be laughing right there with you!"

Boyer finished his pool game and came over to the girls. "Happy New Year, a bit late but still. Joni, I thought you'd be over last night."

Joni shrugged. "Didn't happen. I got lost in the wine and the music." She was thinking, Hmmm, song lyrics. She took out her pen and wrote them in very small letters on her spare coaster.

> *If it takes you to make this happen*
> *Give me music, give me wine*

Boyer stomped off and put another quarter on the pool table, drinking his beer and waiting for his turn to play.

"Come on, Joni," Gina said. "Suck down that beer. I read in the *New Times* that Hans Olson is playing at The Library tonight. I love listening to that guy sing. And I changed into my jeans at work so we could just go right on over."

"Two cars?"

"Sure, in case one of us gets an itch. So why didn't you go to Boyer's last night? Sounds like he was expecting you."

"You know Boyer, he's always up for something, and usually with anybody. He must have been alone and pining for me."

"My butt!" Gina said, laughing. "I can't see Boyer pining for anyone. But he sure seems to have developed an interest in Caffy." She turned around and leaned her head in the direction of the pool table. Caffy was standing by the table and Boyer was showing her how he could bank a ball, but apparently, he was more involved with trying to impress her than to shoot. Not only did he miss the pocket, but he left the cue ball in the perfect position for Pete to make a few easy shots.

"Fine with me. He's fun, but sometimes I get bored with him."

Gina guffawed. "Yeah, I saw him when he streaked The Hut last Halloween. I can't *even* believe you like that."

"Well, as they say, it's not what you got, it's what you do with it."

"Ah, so true, so true. Drink up wench, let's split."

Joni got into her red pickup truck with the camper shell and followed Gina in Pucci to The Library. The parking lot was packed, not unusual when Hans Olson was playing. He was best known for being a solo act who was able to rock a club all night long. And he was incredibly cute, so lots of girls always showed up, Gina and Joni being among that group. Hans had never graced either of their beds, but he always acknowledged their presence at a gig with a nod of his head. Gina thought that made them more friends with Hans than the other groupies. Plus, she loved his music.

Inside, they sat at the bar and ordered a beer. They weren't always as cold at The Library as they were at The Hut, but they did the trick anyway. Gina usually ordered a glass of ice, over which she gently poured her beer. Joni had never picked up the beer-on-ice habit.

Hans was on stage, already tuned, and smiling at the audience.

"Thanks for being here tonight. I hope I can keep your toes rocking for the next few hours." Picking up his beer bottle from the floor and taking a slug, then extending the bottle as a toast to the audience, he said, "I'll be doing a couple of my new original songs that will be on my first album that will be released later this year."

An appreciative murmur from the crowd filled the club.

"You know we'll be picking that up," Gina said. "And I'll be first in line."

"Maybe, if I don't elbow you out of line and cut in!" Joni said. "So, other than listening to Hans, what will we be doing tonight?"

"Did your agency call today?"

"Yep. I have a job at a construction company over in Scottsdale starting tomorrow, so I'm fine with not getting home too late. What about you?"

"I'm into the music and a few more beers. I'm still reeling from the gin I drank with Leroy B. last evening. He'd fill the glass with ice, then pour salt over the ice, and wash it off with gin. Too bad G-I-N is part of my name, because I am way not into it anymore. Maybe let's just listen, have a few beers, and go home."

"Works for me. Even if I didn't unzip my pants on January first—"

Gina butted in. "Except for the multiple times you had to pee."

"Well, there is that. Anyway, I'm fine getting high on the music and taking that to bed with me tonight."

Joni always heard music in her sleep, usually whatever she had listened to that night. Or what she had been singing.

The girls listened to the first set, drank a few more beers, then got ready to leave.

"Hang on, Gina, I gotta pee."

"Joni, the apartment's not fifteen minutes from here."

"Can't wait, Gina, can't wait."

Gina made a face at Joni, then smiled at Joni's back as she walked to the ladies' room.

CHAPTER 3

Friday, January 5. The official memorial for Harry Truman, the thirty-third president of the United States, who died the day after Christmas in 1972 and who led the country through the final days of World War II, was held in Washington, DC. At a bipartisan breakfast meeting with Congressional leaders, Nixon said that he was neither optimistic nor pessimistic regarding the peace negotiations with Vietnam and would do what he regarded as necessary to secure "a proper kind of settlement." The American band Aerosmith releases their debut album, named *Aerosmith*, that included their hit song "Dream On."

· · · · · · · · · · ·

GINA WAS IN THE KITCHEN when Joni got back from her job at the construction company where the temp agency had sent her. She had turned on the radio to KDKB hoping to hear some of the new Aerosmith album.

"Aha," Joni said, pushing the door open and heading toward the kitchen.

"I smelled the liver and onions when I came up the stairs to the breezeway. Boy, are we gonna be healthy today."

"We need to eat, Joni, because I feel a B-I-G party coming on at Peckerwood tonight."

"Why's that, Gina? Just a lot of guys and a lot of kegs and who knows what else down on First Street."

"Well, a *lot* of guys is what I had in mind. More to choose from. Maybe we'll meet some new ones. Pete Groat said that six or seven guys lived there, and if they invite one other boy, that's fourteen guys or if they invite more, well, it could be exponentially interesting."

"You have such a way with words. What are we going to wear?"

"Give it a break, Joni. You always ask that. Pick out one of the shirts your mother made you. It doesn't matter which one since they are all alike anyway. I've told you that more than once!" She laughed. Joni's mother loved to sew. Once she found a pattern that Joni liked, she would sew many shirts with different fabrics using the same pattern. Joni didn't mind.

"Yeah, but I thought I'd branch out tonight."

"Which means you want to wear one of my shirts, right?" Now Gina scowled.

Joni smiled her biggest smile. *"Bingo!"*

"Okay, fine. Get in here and help me with the dinner. All you have to do is turn it over in a few minutes. You can't possibly mess that up. I'll go see what I can find in my closet."

Joni knew that not all the clothing in Gina's closet would be clean, but a bit of perfume would take care of that. Gina's fashion sense was way ahead of Joni's.

"Here," Gina said, holding out a black and red crocheted shawl with black fringe. "I think you wear your black shirt, then you drape this across your shoulders and no one will know you are wearing one of your same old shirts. The fringe will move when you do, so you'll be alluring. Just don't forget to move your arms from time to time."

"What about earrings? What goes with the shawl? What am I going to do?"

"Joni, don't obsess. And turn that meat over or we're going to have burned liver."

Joni did as she was told, noticing that it would have been too late for the liver had Gina not appeared when she did. Skated that one, she thought.

"So, what do I put on my ears?"

"How about my silver earrings with the red hearts in the middle? As long as you think you can get home with *both* of them, Joni. Don't leave them anywhere."

Joni just made a face at Gina, then broke into a smile. She had lost her share of Gina's earrings, or at least one of the earrings in a set, over the years they had been friends. More so since she got to Tempe, because there always seemed to be some kind of insanity going on.

Gina pushed Joni aside, picked up the pan of liver and onions, and placed half on each of their plates, which she had set on the gateleg table by the window. "Sit and eat, Joni dear. And what do you think we should have to start this evening's festivities?"

"A very cold beer, dear! I think Pete Groat said there would be kegs at the party, so let's get started."

"Perfect way to end the workday and get ready to *par-teee*."

With the liver pan in the sink, the dishes on the counter, the ketchup bottle back in the fridge, Joni walked around the living room with the shawl on, practicing moving her arms so the fringe moved in the wind. Gina, purse in hand, walked out of her bedroom and burst out laughing.

"You look like a bird trying to fly, Joni. Just move your arms a bit, don't flap them."

Joni stuck out her tongue at Gina.

"You're driving. We need to take your truck in case we want to crash in the back."

"No problem. I think the truck wants to stop at The Hut first for a pre-party beer."

"Great idea. Let's get going. I can feel a big party coming on."

Joni parked the truck near the front door of The Hut, thinking that she never got a parking space that close. Once inside, the girls discovered why—only three people inside, none of whom the girls knew. Morris was tending bar and as usual, turned his back when he saw the girls. Then he turned around to face them, realizing that he needed their tips this evening with few others in the bar.

"What's happening, Morris?" Gina asked.

"I assume you want your regular pitcher of beer, two glasses, three coasters?"

"Not tonight, Morris honey. Just two draft beers, two coasters."

Joni humphed. Gina was not going to let her doodle on a coaster tonight. Oh well, that was probably for the best so they could get to Peckerwood sooner.

"I guess everyone's at the party down the street," Gina said to Morris.

"My guess is as good as yours," Morris huffed, not being one to chat with the girls and not happy that he wouldn't be making many tips that night.

"Peckerwood must be the place to be. This is our pre-party beer, so serve it up quickly, Morris. If you please." Gina was trying her sweet-talking to get Morris in gear. He pulled on the tap, filled two glasses, and plopped them down in front of the girls. Without coasters.

"Drink up, Joni. I'm certain we'll be more welcome down the street. Peckerwood is calling my name."

"Yep, me too. Leave it to Morris to pour us a warm beer at The Hut. This place has the coldest beer in town." She sucked down her beer in only a few gulps.

"Let's jam, jet, bolt, split, and boogie," Gina said. "Time to get this party going."

The girls waved goodbye to Morris, who ignored them, watching *The Mod Squad* on the new television in the corner instead. Vince would not be happy, as the rule of the bar was that the television was on only for sports events. The girls would never tattle, of course.

Joni pulled onto Second Street, went up a block, and turned right to get to First Street. Then they passed Green Ashes Crematorium where Joe Ravioli worked and the Quonset huts that had been set up right after

WWII to house personnel who were overseeing the prisoner of war camp built at Papago Park.

Driving on, the girls saw flames from what they hoped was a bonfire, not a house on fire, then heard the party. Guitars, singing, and the gentle mumble of a group of happy people.

"Park the truck, Joni. I wanna be at the party."

"I'm trying, Gina. There's so many cars here and I need a place big enough for this vehicle."

"We shoulda brought Pucci. He'd fit anywhere."

Joni just listened and didn't remind Gina that they brought the truck in case they wanted to crash in the back. Gina did this all the time. She could rationalize anything. Joni finally found a space farther down the stone fence, then jumped out and pulled Gina's shawl around her shoulders, glad for the extra warmth on this cool evening.

Walking through the open gate in the stone fence around Peckerwood, the girls headed toward the keg to get some beer. The folk singers were over by the fire, including Leroy B., Joe Ravioli, and Guitar Dave sitting in a circle singing "One Toke Over the Line" by Brewer and Shipley. Behind the singers, in another circle, were other partygoers passing around a joint as they sipped their beer.

"I'm not gonna get in that outer circle," Gina said to Joni. "Smoking a joint just makes me go to sleep and I'm not gonna sleep through this party. Maybe we should have added a white cross to our liver and onions."

"Yes, that might have been a good idea. But I'm so pumped I'm flying on my own adrenaline."

Just then Pete Groat came up behind the girls, taking the arm of each, and said, "Welcome to Peckerwood. Let me show you around." He introduced them to Shotgun Calvin, Rodney, Annie and Jack, Bob and Jill.

Gina had brought a large purse with her and was shifting it around from one shoulder to another. Pete Groat huffed and said, "That's the best part of being a woman. You get to carry a purse and you have control of sex."

The girls laughed at Pete Groat, who waved as he left to join his friends.

"I'm going to go get in the music circle," Joni said to Gina. "I feel a song coming on."

"Fine. I'm going to check out the guys. There must be close to a hundred people here! Mostly *men!*" Gina squealed. "Oh look, there's Max. I've always had a crush on him and been hoping to catch his eye. Maybe this is the night."

"Yep. Good thing they have a large yard," Joni said. "There are certainly a lot of people here, and they are mainly men!"

"Well, I'm gonna see if they have anything else large." Gina showed her dimples and walked toward the beer keg surrounded by four men including Max.

"Hello, I'm Gina, and who are you handsome fellows?"

The men introduced themselves as George and his brother Terry, and an older man named Herbie. Max appeared to be embarrassed by Gina's forward manner and stepped away from the keg, head down.

"Don't mind Max," George said. "He's quite bashful around women."

Gina noticed a quiet man sitting near the house reading a comic book. He was cute, too.

"Who's that guy?" Gina asked George, pointing to the comic-book-reading man.

"That's John-John. He lives under the Mill Avenue Bridge across the Salt River and comes up to party with us and sometimes to bathe."

"The bridge over the Salt? I know that there is rarely any water in the Salt River, but what does John-John do when the river floods?" Gina asked.

"He sleeps in the yard here, or near the crematorium. He does okay for himself. People feed him and buy him beer and everyone gives him their comic books after they read them. John-John loves comic books," Terry said. "You'll see him at The Hut from time to time."

"Wow," Gina said, mouth wide open, then smiling with her fingers in her dimples. "There sure are a lot of interesting *men* here!"

Gina went back to the keg to fill her plastic cup. Joni joined her at the keg and filled her glass.

"Gina, I want to go back to the folk singers. Maybe I'll get up enough nerve to sing with them."

"Fine. I'm going to wander around and see what kind of trouble I can get into!"

Gina walked over toward where Max was standing, and as soon as he saw her, he picked up his beer and walked into the house. Okay, thought Gina, There's more than one fish in the sea. She walked around and saw that Boyer had brought Caffy with him to the party. Well, fine, Joni said she didn't care anyway. Then Gina saw another man leaning against the stone house, slowly drinking his beer, who was also looking right at her. She walked over.

"Hellooooo, I'm Gina," she said, dipping her head to the side and showing her dimples.

"Well, hellooooo back to you, Gina. I'm Gary from Indiana. I live here with Pete Groat."

Gina couldn't contain herself and started singing the song "Gary, Indiana" from one of her favorite musicals, *The Music Man.*

Gary was laughing so hard he almost dropped his beer cup. "Do you think I've never heard that before? But I've never heard it like you sang it."

Gina beamed. "Joni and I—Joni's my roommate— we used to know songs for all fifty states. Well, if we didn't know one we just made it up to the tune of 'Gary, Indiana.'"

"Sing me one about Tempe," Gary said.

"Tempe, Arizona, Tempe, Arizona, Tempe Arizona." Gina sang to the same tune as "Gary, Indiana," then laughed so hard she couldn't continue.

Gary laughed harder this time. "You are so funny! And fun. Let's grab another refill and go into the house. I can show you my etchings."

"I'm up for anything. I hope you are, too... up for anything."

Meanwhile, Joni had made her way to the folk singers and was sitting in between Joe Ravioli and Leroy B. She wasn't sure if she was going to sing, and she hadn't brought her guitar, but surely one of the guys would allow her to use his guitar if she got up enough nerve to sing.

The folk singers were not far from the keg, so everyone took the opportunity to refill their glasses. Joe Ravioli had just returned from the keg with a full glass for him and another one for Joni, when he said, "Okay, guys, time for Joni to sing us one of her songs."

Joni blushed, thinking, Okay, I'm drunk enough to sing but not too drunk to play the guitar.

"Wanna hear a sad song or a funny song?" she asked the group.

She heard mumbles and shouts of "Funny, funny." No one wanted to spoil the mood of the moment.

"Okay, but I'll need to borrow a guitar."

Leroy B. handed over his Martin to Joni, telling her to keep it secure, it was his baby. Joni nodded, fully understanding how precious a Martin guitar was, then sang.

> *I'm just a girl out in the world*
> *I see the guys, they catch my eye*
> *I'm only lookin', I'm not adulterous*
> *Don't hit the town, not going down*
> *No really, I don't fool around*
> *But I hold still while somebody else does*

Everyone was laughing by the time Joni had finished the song. Joni gave the guitar back to Leroy B., and said thank you to all the folk singers and "Time to go home now. What a wonderful evening!" Then she walked toward the keg singing, "Gina, oh Gina, wherefore art thou?"

Gina stumbled out of the house and sang back, "Joni, oh Joni, can you see me now?" It was obvious to Joni that Gina had been drinking maybe a little too much.

Joni took Gina's hand, pulled her toward the truck, and stuffed her into the front seat. By the time they were at the Windbell, Gina was awake enough to walk up to their second-floor apartment. She immediately fell into her bed, fully clothed. Joni just shrugged. At least they had had a good time.

CHAPTER 4

Saturday, January 6. Richard Nixon was officially declared the winner of the 1972 presidential election by Spiro Agnew, the vice president. President Nixon then tells Henry Kissinger that any settlement with North Vietnam would be tolerable. Forty-five B-52s and 115 US fighter-bombers hit targets in North Vietnam. Schoolhouse Rock! premiers on ABC with Multiplication Rock. Both Gina and Joni liked the show and hoped to see it again.

. . . .

JONI WOKE BEFORE GINA, threw on her blue jeans and a T-shirt and trudged up to the office at the apartments to buy a newspaper. Hoping the classifieds would reveal the perfect job for her, Joni put the coins into the newspaper box and pulled out a paper. She stuffed it under her arm and marched back to the apartment, threw the newspaper onto the gateleg table, just missing Gina's potted plant, and turned into the kitchen to put on water for coffee. Joni pulled two coffee cups out of the cabinet, put a spoonful of Kava instant coffee in each, and waited for the teapot to start steaming. She didn't want to wake Gina by having the teapot sing, so she stayed close by.

Filling one cup with water, stirring, then carrying the cup to the gateleg table, Joni picked up the paper and turned to the classified ads. She checked the secretarial jobs first, but nothing was appealing. Reading through all the classifieds, she came across an ad for an evening cocktail waitress at Captain's Beef Rigger on Sixteenth Street in Phoenix. How hard could that be?

Just then Gina shuffled into the living room and plopped down onto the sofa.

"Bring me a coffee, Joni. I'm not sure how much farther than this I am going to go today. Boy, I have no idea how much beer I drank but it may have been more than I needed. So glad you were driving."

"Yeah, we had quite the evening, didn't we?" Joni smiled, remembering the fun, and heated up the water again for Gina, adding cream and sugar to the cup.

"Gina," she said as she handed over the cup. "Check this out—I found a job in the paper I'm going to apply for on Monday. Cocktail waitress at the Captain's Beef Rigger over on Sixteenth Street."

"Joni, you've never been a cocktail waitress. And you are a total klutz. How are you going to pull that off?"

"Well, how hard can it be? The bartender mixes drinks, you put them on a tray and carry them to whoever ordered them. Sounds too easy. Plus, if I smile a lot and wear some of your low-cut shirts, I'll get lots of tips."

"Sounds good in theory, but we shall see how this turns out. You only have three weeks to make the rent, so you'd better find something. That temp agency hasn't been doing so well lately."

"Yep, but they told me that the first week in January was always slow. Maybe next week."

"Give me the rest of the paper and we'll see what's going on in the world. I know you like the news and I don't think I keep up with it enough. So much going on with President Nixon and Vietnam."

Joni threw the paper at Gina and turned on the radio to KDKB. The DJ announced that "You're So Vain" by Carly Simon had just hit number one on the music charts. Then Joni went to clean up the kitchen.

"Hey," Gina shouted into the kitchen. "Today's the twelfth day of Christmas. Woo-eee. Twelve drummers drumming. You know drummers are my favorite." She read on. "And it's also the Epiphany."

"Yeah, I know. The wise men finally get there."

"Sure, but it's more than that, Joni. It symbolizes the end of the Christmas season, but it also is the start of Carnival season that ends with Mardi Gras. Would you rather dress up like three kings on smelly camels or start the Carnival season?"

"I thought you weren't going any farther than the sofa today, Gina."

"A girl can change her mind. Bring me a shot glass of pickle juice, will ya?"

"Pickle juice? Are you nuts?"

"Joni, trust me on this one. My Uncle Jake swore by pickle juice as the way to start curing a hangover, followed by some good old fried eggs. Are there any eggs in the fridge?"

Joni had pulled out the pickles and was trying to pour the juice into the shot glass without spilling too much. She turned to look for eggs and slopped a bit but was sure she could clean it up before Gina noticed. "Yep, there's a few in here. Want me to scramble them up? I'm not sure I could fry them without breaking a yoke."

"Joni, you can't cook worth a damn."

"I know, but how hard can it be to make scrambled eggs?"

"Okay, give it a try. And turn off the radio and put on the TV please."

Joni thought that Gina was a bit over the edge with the hangover card, but she knew better than to say anything about that. Gina was always right. Joni turned on the RCA Trans Vista color television, then went into the kitchen and cleaned up the pickle juice from the counter, pulling out a bowl, the eggs, the whisk, butter, salt, and pepper.

After breakfast, both girls felt much better. Gina read the newspaper that Joni had thrown down onto the coffee table.

"Joni, listen to this. The Hula Bowl and the Senior Bowl are on TV today. We gotta go to The Hut. With that new color TV there, the place should be full of boys."

"I thought we were staying home today," Joni whined.

"Not a chance. We gotta go to The Hut and see what's going on."

Reluctantly, Joni finished washing the dishes and went into her room to get ready. She knew better than to argue with Gina. If Gina wanted them to go to The Hut, they were going to The Hut.

"Will you drive, Gina?" Joni yelled from her bedroom. She was trying to find something to wear. Her clothing from last night smelled like smoke from hanging around the fire.

"Of course, dear Joni. I'm not planning on bringing anyone home who doesn't have *his* own car." She ran into her bedroom to find something enticing to wear.

Once dressed and ready, the girls went to the parking lot at the Windbell and jumped into Pucci. It was a bit cool again, so Gina kept the convertible top up. As they pulled into The Hut, Gina said, "Whoa, see Joni? It's packed. We'll have to park in the alley."

Joni had to admit to herself that maybe they would have a good time today, despite their hangovers.

"Hair of the dog, Gina. Let's just do the hair of the dog. If we get drunk, we'll forget about being hung over."

Gina just laughed.

As the girls expected, The Hut was filled with guys and only a few girls. There was nowhere to sit at the bar. Gina said, "Belly up, Joni. We're going to stand at the bar until some stools become available."

Joni made a face but secretly was glad that she did not wear her wedge shoes, instead opting for her flat-soled boots.

"Good to see you," Florina said to the girls as they stood at the only open space at the bar. "Same as always?"

"Yup. Pitcher of beer and three coasters, please," Gina replied. "And two stools if you have them."

Florina laughed, shaking her head. Just then the two boys to the left of Gina stood up. The dark-haired boy said to Gina, "Please, take our stools. We wouldn't want two such lovely women to be standing while we are just hunkering down on these stools. The only thing is that you will have to allow us to stand by you!"

Gina turned her head sideways, smiled, and stuck her fingers in her dimples. "Oh, you are such a nice boy! Of course you can stand by us!" Gina and the boy started talking to each other, which is when Joni noticed that the blond boy was Vic, the supposed hit man who had been looking for Pilot last year. She remembered that Vic had told her that he had a girl-friend, but if he didn't, he would love to take her home. Joni had hoped that she would never see Vic again, and here he was.

"Hello, Vic," she said to him without smiling.

"Joni, my dear, you are as lovely as ever," Vic said, smiling at her.

"Thank you for the compliment, but what are you doing here? Pilot is long gone and I have no idea where. Or if he is still alive."

"Joni, Joni, Joni. Not to worry about that. As I have heard it, Pilot has been taken care of and he won't be around Tempe anymore."

Joni wasn't sure if anything Vic said was true so just kept her face neutral.

"And Joni, also not to worry about anything else. I am still with my girlfriend and I don't mess around. But seriously, if she ever goes away..."

Joni just kept that thought in her mind, thinking that Vic was really not someone she wanted to deal with. Then he said, "I'm going to play pool. Boyer is over there and he really is pretty good."

Joni took a deep breath and thought, Well, skated that one. She turned to Gina and the other boy, hearing the boy say, "Hello, I'm Graham. I haven't seen you girls here before."

Gina turned to Joni with her eyebrows raised. "What?" she asked, turning back to Graham. "We are here every day and you haven't seen us?"

Graham was smiling and said, "I confess. This is my first time here. Vic wanted me to see the bar with the coldest beer in Tempe. As far as I can tell, he was correct. This beer is great."

"The beer would be even better if there was more of it in our pitcher," Gina said loudly, elbowing Graham and blinking her eyelashes.

"Barkeep," Graham shouted to Florina, "please bring these girls another pitcher of beer if you please. On me." Florina looked at the girls, winked, took their pitcher, and filled it up again. Unless you asked specifically for a fresh one, bartenders at The Hut refilled your glass and your pitcher.

"Graham?" Joni said. "Like a cracker?"

"Actually, yes, like a graham cracker."

"So what do you do, Mr. Graham? You are the first person I know to be named Graham. You must be very special," Gina said, batting her eyelashes again. Joni knew right then and there that Gina wanted to take this little boy home with her tonight.

"What do I do?" An amusing smile slipped across his face. "Well, not much. I'm an independent contractor." Joni narrowed her eyes at this statement. Pilot had been an independent contractor. Jimmy Dick had been an independent contractor. Was that what they were calling drug dealers nowadays?

Graham continued. "But let me tell you about my name. My mother was teaching history at Arizona State University when she learned about the Grahamites, and from that point on she was totally hooked on the name Graham."

"Grahamites?" Gina said with a quizzical look on her face. "What in the world are Grahamites? Bugs?"

Graham laughed. "No, the Grahamites were one of the first vegetarian movements in the US, and graham flour and graham crackers were made just for them. Then there was the Reverend Sylvester Graham who believed that physical lust was bad for the body and caused things like insanity and even headaches and indigestion. This was back in the early 1800s. He also thought that eating mustard and ketchup could cause insanity. He was totally cuckoo but at least we got graham crackers out of it."

Joni had just started listening to what Graham was saying and thought he was making it all up, so she asked, "Well, Graham, what is your *middle* name?"

Graham made a face and pulled up his shoulders. "I really hate this and I think you may be the first person to ask me about this other than when I signed up for the draft." He slugged down half of his beer. "Sylvester."

"Why Graham Sylvester, aren't you the cutest thing in the world today?" Gina butted in so Joni would not have her chance at Graham. She was still not over Joni getting to Wheeler first.

Vic walked back over to the girls, looked at Graham, and said, "Well, seems you are having a better time than I am. That Boyer just won't let anyone else win. I can't tell you how many quarters I have lost to him. I'm ready to go home now so suck up your beer, Graham, and let's get out of here."

"Why, Graham," Gina purred, "if you are not ready to get out of here I would be more than happy to give you a ride home in my car."

Joni thought, Great, now how am I going to get home?

Graham smiled his biggest smile yet and said, "My dear Gina, I would be more than happy to accept your offer for a ride to *your* home." Gina raised her eyebrows, showed her dimples once again, and just beamed.

Joni looked at Vic and said, against her better judgment, "Hey, Vic, can you give me a ride when you leave now? We came in Gina's Fiat Spider and it's pretty small for three people."

Vic grinned. "At your service, Joni."

CHAPTER 5

Monday, January 8. The last US aerial victory of the Vietnam War was scored today by the US Air Force. The trial of the Watergate Seven (Bernard Barker, Virgilio Gonzalez, E. Howard Hunt, G. Gordon Liddy, Eugenio Martinez, James W. McCord Jr., and Frank Sturgis) begins in Washington, DC, presided over by Judge John Sirica. When Joni heard this on the news later in the day, she wondered why people had only initials for their first names.

· ·

THE PHONE RANG AT 7:00 a.m. Gina could sleep through anything, but Joni heard it and rushed out of bed into the living room to answer the beige Princess phone. It was her temp agency. "A job? Doing what? . . . And where is it? . . . Okay. Typing for a plumbing company over on Twelfth Street. Perfect. . . . I'll take it. Eight to five?"

Joni took a ten-minute shower, rousted Gina out of bed with a cup of coffee, and said, "The temp agency called. I'm going to type at a plumbing company over on Twelfth Street. Regular hours, so I'll just go from there over to Captain's Beef Rigger to interview for the cocktail waitress job. What should I wear?"

Gina yawned. "You really are not a cocktail waitress, but what the hey. And you could wear that blue dress your mother made you with your blue shoes. Cute enough."

Joni hurried to her closet, pulled her underwear out of the boxes in the closet that served as her dresser drawers, found a pair of hose without a run, and was ready to go.

"Why don't you come on over to the Beef Rigger when you get off work. If nothing else, we can have a drink in a new place."

"Sure, why not? It's only a few blocks out of my way home."

"Fingers crossed I get the job," Joni said, crossing her fingers.

"Break a leg, Joni." Gina, as a former drama student, had heard that line many times.

Joni typed invoices all day long for drain repairs, stopped-up toilets, and dripping faucets. It was all she could do to stay awake. Plumbing was not her favorite thing. At least she was typing and not having to dig around in people's pipes. Five o'clock came and she turned off her typewriter, smiled, and said goodbye to the office manager, who said, "Joni, could you come back and work tomorrow?"

Joni smiled, nodded her head, and rushed out to her truck. She was off to Captain's Beef Rigger, a large Arizona-style adobe and timber building.

Parking in the employee designated area, Joni remembered to comb her hair as Gina had advised. Joni was always forgetting to comb her hair. Jumping out of the car, Joni went to the front door and asked for Patty as the ad stated. The maître d' took Joni's arm and escorted her to the employee area of the restaurant. Patty arrived just as Joni was tripping over the leg of the folded chair set up for the interview. Patty pretended not to notice, thinking, Who needs a clumsy person for a waitress?

Joni stuck her hand out for a shake, smiling, just as Patty said, "The job's been filled. You can leave your résumé with me in case we need someone in the future."

Joni shrugged. "Okay. Thanks for your time." She hadn't remembered to take a résumé with her. Besides, it would just say she typed one hundred words per minute. The only waitress job she held was just out of high school, serving coffee and tea and hot chocolate at The Rubaiyat, a folk club in Dallas where she met Jerry Jeff Walker and Michael Martin Murphey and Donny Brooks when they were still struggling young musicians, all of whom went on to become famous. They were playing for ten dollars a night back then. Joni dropped the plastic glasses so often the folk singers started asking for her not to serve drinks while they were singing, but the owner liked her so she got to stay for a few months before going off to college.

Walking out of the employee area through the two connected dining rooms toward the cocktail dining lounge, Joni heard a male voice singing a John Prine song she loved. She asked the maître d' who was playing, and he replied, "Tom Dixon. He plays here for happy hour on Mondays"—he pointed to the left— "over in the lounge."

Joni walked in that direction just as Gina came in the front door.

"So, short interview?"

"Job's filled, but listen to the folk singer. Buy you a drink?"

"Sure. Can't dance." Both of them walked into the darkness of the lounge, where they saw a sandy-blond-haired guy with a Martin guitar in his lap, just ending the song. He looked up, saw the girls, smiled, and said, "Welcome to the Beef Rigger lounge."

No one else was in the lounge other than the waitress, who came over as soon as the girls sat down.

"Happy hour special, double shots for one dollar. The buffet over there is free. What'll it be?"

"John Collins for both of us," Gina said. As the waitress left to get their order, she said to Joni, "And there's our dinner," pointing to the buffet. "Let's see what's on that table. I can't believe they have all this food and double shots for a dollar."

They found little sausages in barbecue sauce, cubes of cheese, crackers, celery, carrots, and another hot, covered serving dish with what looked to be mini egg rolls when the lid was raised.

"M-m-m-m-m," said Gina. "What more could a young girl want?"

Joni couldn't argue, piling her plate full as the only thing she had for lunch was a cup of Lipton's instant pea soup. In her purse, Joni carried a portable immersion water heater that she just stuck in a cup of water, plugged in at her desk wherever she was working, then when the water started boiling, took out the heater and added the packet of soup. Cheap and easy. Joni also believed that hot pea soup was another way to cure a hangover.

The girls sat down at their table just as the waitress delivered their drinks and as the folk singer was finishing up Gordon Lightfoot's "Early Morning Rain." He set his guitar on the guitar stand and said, "A small pause for the cause. Be back in a few minutes."

Then he walked over to the girls' table and sat down, saying to them, "Hi," looking first to Gina and next to Joni where his eyes lingered for a few seconds. "I'm Tom Dixon. I play here every Monday for happy hour. Tuesdays and Thursdays I do happy hour over at the Fireside Lounge. First time here? I don't think I've seen you before."

Joni just smiled at him. Gina said, "Yep. Joni thought she would apply for a waitress job here, but they said it was filled." Then laughing, she said, "Which is probably the best thing for the Beef Rigger because Joni's a klutz and can't keep from breaking glasses and dishes anyway."

Tom Dixon looked at Joni to see how she was taking all this, but Joni had already started laughing with Gina.

"Way it is," Joni said. "Just the way it is."

The trio talked for a few moments, then Tom Dixon went to get ready for his next set. He stood up, took a few steps toward the stage, then turned around and said, "Hope to see you tomorrow at the Fireside Lounge for happy hour," looking directly at Joni as he talked.

You can count on it, Joni thought.

"Well," Gina said. "Looks like you've met another new man this year. He kinda likes you."

"Works for me. Should we stop at The Hut on the way home or just go rest and get ready for Tuesday?"

"I could use the rest," Gina said. "Besides, I want to see that *All in the Family* show. It's pretty amazing that they have this bigoted guy on there with the hippie daughter. You never know where that show is going next."

"Works for me. I've certainly had enough to eat and this double John Collins gave me a buzz. I'll follow you home."

CHAPTER 6

Tuesday, January 9. The Vietnam War peace talks moved closer to a resolution when Henry Kissinger and a Vietnamese revolutionary general reached a tentative agreement in Paris. The South Vietnamese government was opposed to this tentative agreement.

• •

THE GIRLS WOKE EARLY AND refreshed. Joni was in the shower, listening to Gina singing, "It's *T* for Tuesday, *T* for you and me. It's *T* for Tuesday, will we get luck-ee ... ?"

"Gina, are we gonna come home first and change clothing, or what?"

"Joni, we're going to go from work to the Fireside Lounge and listen to Tom Dixon sing. Then we'll figure it out."

"Oh, yeah. Guess I spaced that out."

"Amazing, since your eyes undressed him a few times last night."

"I thought only guys did that to girls."

"Right, Joni! Hurry up. We need to get to work on time so we can leave right at five tonight. Who knows what the Fireside has to offer a young girl. We can go in one car; I'll drop you off at the plumbing shop. It's not too far out of the way to downtown Phoenix where I work."

The day passed with the girls calling each other only a few times. They lived together, they played together, and they still talked as often as they could. Forever friends, they called it.

Finally, five o'clock and time to leave work. Joni stood outside the plumbing office waiting for Gina who pulled up in Pucci, her orange Fiat Spider, top still up with the unseasonably cool temperatures. Pucci turned the corner on Eleventh Street and headed toward the plumbing office. Joni jumped in.

The Fireside Lounge was only a few blocks away. Gina parked near the front door and told Joni to comb her hair. Joni made a face at Gina but pulled a comb from her purse. "You are obsessed with me combing my hair."

"Because you don't comb your hair, silly girl. You wanna look good for Tom Dixon, right?"

Tom Dixon was already singing when the girls walked in the lounge. It was dark, with a few people sitting at tables. The girls sat as near to the stage as they could. To the right of the stage they saw a blond, long-haired boy turning the knobs on what appeared to be the PA system.

"Wow," Gina said. "Look at that. Cute, cute, cute. If he goes along with the folk singer, we have a package deal here."

When Tom Dixon finished his set, the blond, long-haired boy turned off the PA and turned on the canned music. He walked over to the girls. "Hi, my name's Benson. Hope you're enjoying the show."

"You're Ben's son?" Gina said, sticking her fingers in her dimples and leaning her head to the right. "Who's Ben?"

Benson laughed. "You are so funny! Just Benson, my whole first name. What's your name, little lady?"

"Gina. And this is Joni. We met Tom Dixon yesterday at the Captain's Beef Rigger when Joni was over there looking for a job."

"Yes," Benson said, "they go through waitresses there like water."

Joni watched as Tom Dixon set his guitar on the guitar stand, then turned to talk to a girl who had walked up to the stage. Gina was absorbed in Benson, whose fingers were filled with rings of turquoise and silver, a silver chain around his neck with a turquoise drop.

"Yeah, but not to worry. Joni can't get a dish from the table to the sink without dropping or spilling something. She can type like a banshee, but she can't handle dishes. It's just as well for the world that she didn't get the job." She took a sip of her John Collins. "But we did get to meet Tom Dixon and now, we get to meet *you!*"

"At your pleasure," Benson said, sitting down at the girls' table.

Tom Dixon was walking with a girl to another table, Joni staring intently at him.

"So," Gina continued. "What do you do?" Gina knew that this was not something you asked strangers you just met, but she had to do it. She liked the looks of this guy.

"I run sound for Tom Dixon when I can. Other than that, I deal in silver and turquoise jewelry. Tom Dixon likes it when I'm doing the sound and making sure he sounds good."

"Well, Joni thinks he sounds good." Gina nodded her way. "And she thinks he looks good, too!"

"As do you, my lovely Gina. Maybe we could get together sometime and discuss the state of affairs in the world."

"Affairs?" said Gina, raising her eyebrows and smiling. "I don't do married men."

Benson laughed. "I'm not married, you silly girl. The affairs of the *world*! What's going on, showing you my etchings . . . you know . . ." Yes, Gina did remember the last time someone had asked her to see his etchings, and it had been wonderful.

Gina blushed, something she was able to do on command. Benson fell for it and smiled.

Tom Dixon finished talking with the other girl and walked over to the table with Benson, Gina, and Joni.

"So glad you could join us tonight. Did you find the Fireside to your liking?" he asked.

"I found your soundman to my liking," Gina said, tilting her head again and smiling at Benson.

"Gina, you are so bad," Joni said, finally taking her eyes off Tom Dixon.

Tom Dixon laughed. "Have you girls tried the buffet here? I think it's even better than the one at Captain's Beef Rigger."

"We're more into the music tonight," Gina said. "And we like Ricky Nelson, if you know any."

"Yes," Joni said, "and also John Prine. We heard you sing one the other night, about hauling your ashes."

Tom Dixon smiled and said, "I like that song a lot. Love the double entendre of hauling your ashes."

The girls' faces showed that they did not know the reference. "What?" he continued. "You've never heard that expression? It's about sex!" A grin spread across his whole face.

"Well, we'll just have to try that sometime," Gina drawled in her best Texas accent. She looked directly at Benson, who was grinning about as big as Tom Dixon was.

"Time for another set," Benson said to Tom. "We'll see you girls later."

Gina looked at Benson and said, "We're going to The Hut. It's sixty-five-cent pitcher night. Plus, music at The Cave and twenty-five-cent tequila. Over on Mill Avenue in Tempe. Wanna join us?"

Both boys raised their eyebrows, Tom Dixon saying, "Maybe so. We'll see what happens." He stood up and walked toward the stage, then turned back to look at the girls once more. He started the set with "Hello Mary Lou" by Ricky Nelson.

The girls finished their drinks to the Ricky Nelson tune, then nodded at the boys before leaving the Fireside and jumping into Pucci.

"We'd better go home and change, Joni. I feel another big evening coming on and I don't want to spend it in my work clothes."

"Sure thing. You're driving, I'm just along for the ride."

"And quite the ride it's been since you arrived here last year." Both girls were thinking about their adventures. "And I hope that Tom Dixon and Benson are part of our adventures this year. They're both so cute."

"Hard to tell how cute Benson is with all that silver and turquoise on him, Gina."

"Yep. Part of his charm, for sure."

After a quick stop at the apartment to change clothes, Gina and Joni hurried to The Hut. They walked through the door to hear the jukebox playing "Don't Let Me Be Lonely Tonight" by James Taylor and the Paul Bunyan pinball machine ringing bells and whistles as Craig from Colorado tried to beat the house. Gambling was not allowed in Arizona, but the bar paid off in nickels for the pinball machine. Vince knew that the nickels would just go right back to the bar for more pitchers of beer, so it all worked out for him.

Boyer and Joe Ravioli were playing pool with Caffy looking on.

"Looks like Boyer has hooked that little girl," Gina said.

"Fine with me. He was too into a one-on-one relationship for my tastes anyway."

Morris was tending bar, ignoring the girls once again. Florina, however, was on the drinking side of the bar and yelled at Morris to get the girls their pitcher of beer and to bring it to the stools next to her. He snorted, but obliged, knowing that Florina hired the bartenders and he still had two semesters of school to pay for.

"Hey, Florina, what's going on around here?" Gina asked.

"Oh, same old, same old, except check this out. We have a new game. Ship, Captain, Crew," Florina said, shaking the dice cup.

"Is it like Horses?" Horses was a bar game Gina and Joni learned from Florina last year. The game was a lot like poker but played with dice, and the loser had to put money in the jukebox even if the loser was the bar.

"Not quite. You need to roll a six, which is a 'ship,' a five, which is the 'captain,' and a four, which is the 'crew.' You get up to three rolls to do this and the dice left over are your score. Highest score wins; loser puts money in the jukebox."

"Let me do it," Gina said. "I got the luck."

Joni only nodded. Gina was always winning something.

"*Aha!* Ship, first roll." Gina shook the cup again. "Captain. *Ha ha!*" Then another roll to get her crew.

Florina rolled for the bar and lost. Pushing fifty cents Gina's way, she said, "Play me something good. I'll have Morris bring you another pitcher."

Pete Groat walked in as Gina was heading toward the jukebox. "Hi Pete Groat," Gina said, handing him the money for the jukebox. "I just won at Ship,

Captain, Crew. Why don't you play the songs? Florina wants something good."

"Sure thing, little lady." Pete took the coins and shoved them into the slot. Pushing the buttons for "You Ought to Be With Me" by Al Green, and "Sweet Surrender" by Bread, he was thinking maybe the girls would get the drift of his choices. He waved hello to Caffy, then walked up to the girls. "And what are the Mill Avenue Hussies up to tonight?"

Gina smiled. "Waiting for two guys to come walking through the door and sweep us off our feet."

"Does one count?" Pete said, pointing at himself with everyone laughing. The girls had already talked about Pete Groat and they knew he was going to be one of their friends, like Joe Ravioli had become. Pete liked to laugh, and laughing was first on the girls' agenda for a good time.

Pete Groat had just started drinking his first glass of beer when the front door to The Hut opened and in walked Benson and Tom Dixon.

"Aha," Gina said, swooning and wiping her forehead, "my feet are already off the floor."

Benson and Tom Dixon smiled as they walked back to where the girls were sitting. Pete looked at the girls and shook his head, saying, "I'm going to play pool now. Catch you down the line." He walked over to the pool table to join Boyer and Caffy.

Touching Gina on the shoulder, Benson said, "So glad to see you here. We don't get over to Tempe much and look forward to having you show us around." Then to Morris, who was trying his best to ignore the group, "How about one of the sixty-five-cent pitchers of beer we've heard so much about? And two more glasses, please."

Morris shrugged, sneered at the girls, then turned to draw the pitcher of beer. Tom Dixon sat on the stool next to Joni and smiled at her. Joni smiled back.

"Howdy doo, Tom Dixon," Gina shouted across Joni. "How's it hangin', left or right?"

"Doing great, Gina," he answered, "but I'm not sure about the left or right thing. I can assure you, however, that it's hanging!"

"Don't bother with Gina's question," Joni said. "Our friend Koo once told us that right-handed men dressed to the left and left-handed men dressed to the right. That tailors would build extra space in custom-made trousers to accommodate, well, you know what. The Hut was full that night and we were pretty loose, so we walked up and down the bar and did a test study for every man who was standing up. Turns out Koo was right."

Benson's eyes widened. "You mean you walked up and down this bar," tapping the bar top, "and put your hand down men's pants?"

Gina laughed. "Not down their pants, silly boy. Just between their leg, like this." She patted her hand between Benson's legs. "Hmmm, a southpaw."

"Well, I'll be. You are right," Benson said.

To Tom Dixon only, Joni said, "I know you are right-handed because I've seen you play guitar. I'll pass on the test."

"Maybe it's something we could get to later," Tom Dixon said, eyes sparkling, a smile turning up the corners of his mouth ever so slightly.

Well, that certainly would float my boat, Joni thought, raising her eyebrows in a smile.

Setting her glass down on the bar with a slap, Gina pronounced, "Pitcher's empty, tequila's calling. Let's walk down the street and see what we can find."

The boys emptied their glasses, each putting a hand on the back of his respective partner, and the group walked to the front door.

The foursome walked out the front door of The Hut and turned on Mill Avenue to find some more action. The Cave looked to be full of bikers, so they continued on to Parry's. The music was playing, and there was no cover that night. They found a table close to the bar.

"To-kill-ya or beer?" Benson asked the others.

"Beer for me," Gina and Joni said at the same time.

"One tequila for me," Tom Dixon said.

"Coming right up!" Benson said. Gina was thinking, Yup, hope you are coming right up . . .

After their drinks arrived, Tom Dixon asked Joni to dance. Joni loved to dance and so far had found that not many men liked it as much as she did. She beamed and lifted her hand for Tom Dixon to assist her out of her chair. Gina and Benson stayed at the table, talking and holding hands.

Another round and everyone agreed that it was time to go back to the Windbell. Benson rode with Gina. Tom Dixon took Joni's hand and pulled her to his car, not even waiting until the door was closed before he swooped in for a kiss.

Just after 2:00 a.m., Tom Dixon told Joni that he had to go. He knocked softly on the door to Gina's bedroom and let Benson know that he was going. Benson asked for a minute and soon appeared fully clothed. The boys left the apartment with Gina and Joni waving goodbye shyly.

"See you later, alligator," Gina said softly, using the phrase she had previously reserved for Joni.

"In a while, crocodile," Benson replied.

Gina blushed. That was her and Joni's shtick. But she was fine sharing it with Benson.

CHAPTER 7

Tuesday, January 16. Corning Glass Works was granted a patent for optical fiber on this day, changing tele-communications forever. Warmer weather relieved the fuel crisis across the US.

. . . .

IT WAS A TUESDAY, WHICH meant a Hut night, but the girls were staying home to watch the 440th and final showing of *Bonanza*. Gina had a crush on Adam. Joni had a crush on Little Joe. Gina had made rumaki for them to enjoy while they watched the show.

"You know what, Gina?" Joni said. "I never really liked chicken livers until you served them to me this way. What a treat."

"Yup, they are basically water chest-nuts and pieces of chicken liver wrapped in bacon and marinated in soy sauce with brown sugar. I'm sure the chicken livers are healthy enough to counter the fat in the bacon. Plus, they are so yummy."

When the show was over, the girls looked at each other and neither one of them really wanted to go out and party.

"What in the world was this ending?" Joni asked. "Where was Hoss? Why wasn't the ending more spectacular?"

"Well, Joni, I read that Dan Blocker who played Hoss died suddenly so he wasn't able to be in this episode. I guess the writers had to rethink it."

"But why did Little Joe have to get so nasty?" Joni added.

"He's a guy, isn't he?" Gina shrugged like this was the answer to all strange questions. "At least the show was in color so we could take advantage of my RCA Trans Vista color television. Joni, get me a shot of brandy. I think it's time to wind this evening down."

Joni poured Gina a shot of brandy, adding one for herself.

CHAPTER 8

Thursday, January 18. South Vietnam indicated that the idea of peace is not completely welcome. Saigon feels that peace is very near between the US and North Vietnam, but some in South Vietnam suspect the US of selling them out. In Vietnam this week, US losses include 2 dead, 6 missing in action, and 11 wounded. South Vietnam had 476 dead and claims to have killed 1,757 enemy troops.

. . . .

JONI WAS UP EARLY BECAUSE her stomach hurt and she was terribly constipated. She decided to try a remedy her grandmother had given to her and went into the kitchen, trying to be quiet so Gina could sleep a little more. Apparently, she did not succeed as she accidentally banged the saucepan on the stove.

"Joni, what in the world are you doing?" Gina yelled.

"Stewing prunes. My grandmother said that they have many properties and you should eat them every day, especially if you are constipated."

"Joni, you know you can't cook."

"Yeah, well, but how hard can it be to put prunes and water in a pan and boil them until the prunes are soft. Besides, my grandmother lived to be one hundred years old."

Gina shook her head. "I just can't believe this. Why is your stomach backed up?"

"Who knows. Maybe it was the cheese crisps we had at the Dash Inn last night after we went to The Hut."

"Joni, you did have three cheese crisps. I think one serving is only one cheese crisp."

"I was hungry," Joni argued.

"Yes, and now I'm going to have to listen to you tell me how much weight you gained. Anyway, I had a boyfriend from India whose grandfather drank a cup of his own urine every morning so he could stay regular. He lived to be ninety-eight. What do you think about that?"

Joni pondered. "Well, I think that prunes beat piss by two years." She turned to stir the prunes in the pan.

"Are you working today?" Gina asked. "Did your temp agency find you something to do? Rent's coming up, you know."

"I'm sure they will find me something. You'll have to drive yourself to work. I'll take whatever they have open."

Gina readied for work and sent Joni an air kiss as she walked out the door of their apartment. At eight o'clock the phone rang, and Joni ran to pick it up.

"Hello? Is this my agency?" Joni said, anticipating a job offer.

"Yes, it is. I have one opening today in Chandler if you don't mind driving that far. It's answering the phones in the lobby at a bank. You have to sit at your desk all day and are only allowed breaks every two hours."

"I'll take it," Joni said, thinking, Oh boy, as often as I have to go to the bathroom, how am I going to sit for two hours in the lobby of a bank?

Joni got directions to the bank from the temp agency and hurried to be ready. The bank did not open until nine so she had time to get to the location. Joni did not allow herself a cup of coffee or even a glass of water and knew that she was going to get wrinkles from no hydration. But oh well, a job was a job.

That afternoon, Joni had a lull in answering the phones and called Gina at work.

"Hey, I'm at a bank in Chandler answering telephones. And they only allow you to pee once every two hours. I haven't had anything to drink all day and have to be here until six p.m. Meet you at The Hut after that?"

Gina smiled at her end of the conversation. "Nope, I'll go home after work and you just meet me there when you can. I have a surprise for you!"

"A surprise?" Joni shouted, which caused one of the bank tellers to look her way and admonish her with her scowl. "Gotta go, Gina. The bank people are making funny faces at me."

"See you soon," Gina said in her singing voice.

The afternoon dragged on forever for Joni. She was thinking that working in a bank was not what she wanted to do, but as Gina had said, the rent was due and she had to deal with it. At 6:00 p.m., Joni put the phones into night mode, pulled her purse from the drawer in the desk where she had been sitting all day, and headed toward the ladies' room before she drove back to Tempe. It was just over ten miles and this was in the end of rush hour traffic, so maybe it wouldn't be too bad.

"Lucy," Joni shouted as she walked in the door to their apartment, "I'm home." Gina laughed, as Joni and she often used that line from the *I Love Lucy* show.

"I'm in the bedroom. Get yourself a beer and have a seat on the sofa."

Joni wondered what was up. Then Gina waltzed into the living room and said, "Joni, I got us a dog."

"What? Dogs are not allowed here and even if they were, we couldn't afford a pet deposit. And who is going to take care of it when we are at work? Or drinking? Or partying?"

Gina laughed, her dimples showing. She gestured with her left hand sweeping behind her and said, "Joni, meet Space Dog. You're going to love him. He can go wherever we go."

Joni saw nothing behind Gina, then looked at her smiling face and knew what it was. *"An invisible dog!"*

"Yup, you got it in one try! We can take him wherever we want, he can go wherever he wants, and no one needs to know. Plus, just think of what we will save on dog food."

"Gina, you are so bad!"

The girls had always been in touch with each other on so many levels. Joni knew just where Space Dog was and walked over to pet him. "Ah, Gina, this is such a treat!"

"And, because I knew you would want to stay here and play with him, I brought us a gallon jug of Gallo red wine, the same wine we get to go to the Tempe park and listen to music. We'll have our own party tonight here at the Windbell."

Just then the phone rang. It was Joni's temp agency.

"Joni, the bank wasn't overly impressed with you, so they are asking for another temp tomorrow. I do have a job filing at a real estate company. Are you up for that?"

"Sure," Joni answered. "Just give me the address and I'll be there." She hung up the phone.

"Well, Joni, that sounded like your agency has a job for you tomorrow. More money, more fun, and we won't have to move. Woo-hoo!"

Joni looked at Gina and smiled, then reached out and petted Space Dog. "Let me get you another glass of wine."

CHAPTER 9

Friday, January 19. As usual, President Richard Nixon went to the Kennedy Center to hear the Philadelphia Orchestra. The closing selection was the *1812 Overture*, often considered to be the divine military orchestral piece. Several members of the Philadelphia Orchestra asked to be released from the performance because of the Vietnam War, and their requests were not approved. The event proceeded as scheduled.

· · · · · · · · · · · · · · · · · · · ·

AS USUAL, JONI AND GINA met at The Hut after work. They arrived at the same time and parked next to each other in the back. It was not unusual for the girls to be at the same place at the same time. Part of the forever friends thing. They almost always seemed to be on the same wavelength. Space Dog had gone to work with Gina, and he wasn't with her at The Hut.

"Where's Space Dog?" Joni asked.

"He wanted out this morning at the Salt River. He let me know that he would be at our apartment when we got there tonight."

"So whaddya want to do?" Joni asked Gina as they waited for their pitcher of beer to be poured. "I worked my buns off today doing filing at some wretched real estate company and by filing, I don't just mean paper. They had me hauling boxes of files from one room to another so I'm ready for some R&R."

"Joni, Joni, you are so lame. Hans Olsen is playing at The Library tonight and we have to go see him."

"Well, Hans is always a good reason to find my second wind, so let's finish this pitcher and head on out. We can just wear our work clothes tonight. And, I think taking two cars is the best since I am really tired and you might find something that hits your fancy."

Gina laughed. "Hits my fancy? Like you hit the light pole last year when Pilot loaned you his Celica?" She downed her glass of beer, filling it again with the last beer from their pitcher, which she then sucked down. "Let's go, wench!"

The Library was packed as the girls walked in and Hans Olsen had just started his set. He saw the girls and nodded his head their way. The girls smiled. Hans had become a good friend.

No barstools remained empty at the bar, so the girls ordered their drinks and went to find a table. The only available chairs were at a table where a young blond man sat.

"Oh, hello, you handsome devil," Gina said. "Are you expecting company because here we are!"

He looked at Gina, then at Joni, and shrugged. "Well, I guess two girls are better than one," he responded. "I'm Teddy."

"Oh, my," Gina replied, fanning herself with her hand. "Teddy Bear, I suppose?"

He laughed and said, "Just Teddy, but if you want to call me Teddy Bear that's fine with me."

The girls sat down at the table. Teddy asked Gina to dance, and Joni stayed at the table, drinking her beer. When the dance was over and Teddy and Gina returned to the table, Joni said, "Gina, I wasn't kidding about needing to rest after working so hard today. Okay if I go home now?"

Gina looked at Joni with a gleam in her eye. It was obvious to Joni that Gina thought Teddy Bear was just the thing for her to sleep with tonight. "Sure, Joni. See you when I get home."

Joni left and drove to the Windbell and just as Gina said, Space Dog was waiting for her in the living room.

CHAPTER 10

Saturday, January 20. Richard Nixon and Spiro Agnew were inaugurated at the US Capitol, their second and last inauguration. Both Nixon and Agnew resigned before the end of their second term.

• • • • • • • • • • • • • • • • • • • •

"WAKE UP, JONI," GINA SAID, shaking the posts of the bed Joni was given by a woman at one of the temp places she had worked and rocking the bed from side to side.

"Gee-zus, Gina, what do you want? It's not even six a.m."

"That boy stole my car, Gina."

"Pucci's gone? Are you sure?"

Gina stopped shaking the bed and said, "After The Hut we went to his house and then I wanted to come home because I could barely stand up so he said he would drive. I thought, Sure, what does it matter whose bed we fall into? Then when we pulled into the parking lot here at the Windbell, I opened the car door and grabbed my purse. Then he just took off with Pucci. Oh, Joni, what am I going to do?"

Joni was silent for a moment, then said, "We need to go to the police, Gina. We need to tell them Pucci was stolen." She pulled herself up off the bed and walked out of her bedroom into the bathroom, thinking, Good thing I passed out with my clothes on because now I don't have to get dressed.

Joni drove Gina to the Tempe police station in her pickup truck. It was a quick ride at that time of the morning down Broadway to Mill Avenue and on to 120 E. Fifth Street.

"Pull it together, Gina. We both may still be drunk but we don't want to appear that way at the station."

Joni pulled into the police station parking lot. The girls smoothed their hair and straightened their clothing as best they could. Walking inside, they went to the policeman sitting behind the front desk who looked at them a long time before saying, "Girls, what can I do for you?"

"Someone stole my car," Gina said. "A guy was driving me home and when I got out of the car, he took off with it."

"When did this happen?" the policeman asked.

"This morning about six a.m.," Gina said.

"Well, I think it best if you girls just go home and wait ten days to see if he shows up again with your car. There's nothing we can do until then," he said, looking down at the report he was reading when the girls walked in and not paying any more attention to the girls.

"But..." Gina said.

"Gina," Joni interrupted, "let's just go home and come back in ten days." Gina didn't want to go, but Joni gave her "the look" and Gina knew it was time to get out of the police station.

"Do you think he knew we were still drunk?" Gina said as the girls walked back to Joni's truck.

"I hope not. At least it is the weekend and we don't have to go to work today. I already have enough saved up for next month's rent."

The girls went home, changed out of last night's clothing, and put on their granny dresses. Gina went right to bed. Joni made them coffee. It was a long day and the girls just wanted to be left alone. Joni locked the front door. The girls stayed in the apartment with the door locked until Monday morning.

CHAPTER 11

Monday, January 22. The United States Supreme Court delivers its decisions in *Roe v. Wade* and *Doe v. Bolton*, legalizing elective abortion in all fifty states.

• •

JONI HAD WORKED OVERTIME AT the accounting firm where her temp agency had sent her that day, and wanted nothing more than to go home and rest. Gina was riding to work and back with Joni and wanted to go to The Hut. Joni knew that Gina needed extra pampering so drove straight to The Hut, parking in the back.

"Anything exciting happening, Florina?" Joni said, entering through the back door of The Hut.

"Nothing much. I've already got your pitcher and glasses set up right there in the middle of the bar." They were sitting along with the extra coaster Joni used for her doodling and song lyrics.

"You girls are late today. What's with that?" Florina asked.

"Working overtime," Joni said. "I never mentioned to my temp agency that I really didn't know how to operate a ten-key machine so maybe it took me longer to do my work than anyone else. Maybe I didn't even know what a ten-key machine was, but I took the job anyway. I asked the temp agency not to send me to any more accounting firms."

Florina just laughed as Gina picked up her beer glass and emptied it, saying, "Drink up, Joni. You get the last glass from this pitcher and I am ready to go home."

"Me too," Joni agreed. "But what are we going to eat?"

"You are always focused on food, Joni. Let's make this easy and just have grilled cheese sandwiches and tomato soup. Even you can do that without making too much of a mess."

Joni emptied the pitcher into her beer glass, then sucked it down.

"Ciao for now," Joni said to Florina, waving as the girls left The Hut. Gina was extra quiet.

Once back at the Windbell, Joni opened the can of tomato soup and poured it and a can of milk into a pan to heat, stirring it with the whisk Gina loved to use. Then she tried her best to make the grilled cheese sandwiches for Gina and herself. By the end of Joni's "cooking," the kitchen was a mess. Gina just shook her head and walked to her bedroom, waiting for Joni to bring the soup and sandwich to her. *Rowan & Martin's*

Laugh-In was on, and Gina wanted to watch it on the TV in her bedroom.

Joni brought the soup and sandwich in to Gina and sat on the edge of the bed to watch the show with Gina. Afterward, Joni spent an hour cleaning the kitchen and watched the late evening news in the living room on the RCA Trans Vista color television. Joni did not have a TV in her room.

Space Dog decided that Gina needed him to sleep in her bed that night.

CHAPTER 12

Tuesday, January 23. President Nixon announces that a peace accord had been reached in Vietnam.

• • • • • • • • • • • • • • • • • • • •

GINA AWOKE DECLARING THAT SHE was ready for "*T* for Tuesday" and was looking forward to them going to The Hut after work. The night of rest seemed to ease her pain over losing her car.

"Joni," Gina yelled into the kitchen while fixing her hair, "do you have a temp job today? The rent is due in a week and I'm not even thinking about having to move because you can't pay your share."

"No job yet, but I'll get on the phone at eight a.m. Even if I have to go to the accounting firm again. Yuk."

"Which means that you can't take me to work today. I'll take a taxi, so no worries. Call me later so I can figure out how to get home."

Joni called the temp agency at 8:00 a.m. and found that they had one job available, a housekeeping job at the Holiday Inn on East Apache in Tempe. Joni was sure she knew how to make a bed so accepted the job and got ready for work. Gina had already taken the cab to her job at the insurance company.

It was quite the surprise for Joni. First, she had to wear a really ugly uniform that didn't fit. Joni thought she may need to diet and grow a larger chest area in order to fill out this uniform. And then most of the other housekeepers didn't speak English, which made their trying to teach Joni how to make a bed properly not the easiest of tasks. But Joni did her best and earned her money and in the late afternoon changed back into her own clothes.

Calling Gina, she sang, "I'll be down to get you in a taxi, honey."

Gina laughed, maybe the first time since Pucci had been stolen. "I assume that means you will be coming to pick me up at work."

"Yup," Joni said, smiling as she was so happy to hear Gina laughing again.

Florina served up a pitcher and two glasses quickly when she saw the girls arrive. The Hut was quiet that night, not many men around, neither friends nor frat boys, so the girls decided they would just go home and watch television. The TV offerings were slim, but the girls found one they liked, "The Flight of the Snow Geese." The story was about the majestic beauty and spirit of the snow goose on its annual flight from Canada to the Gulf of Mexico, with the theme song being "Fly High and Free," which was sung by Glen Campbell.

"'Fly High and Free,'" Gina said. "Just like I've always said to you. The way we need to be." And then she drifted off to sleep on the sofa.

CHAPTER 13

January 30. Another Tuesday. Joni liked to listen to the news as she drove to work and on the way to The Hut after work. She picked up Gina, then heard that G. Gordon Liddy and James W. McCord Jr., former aides to President Nixon, had been convicted of conspiracy, burglary, and wiretapping in the Watergate incident. Joni had grown up in a tight Christian family and didn't understand how politicians could be so corrupt. Maybe that would change as time went on, Joni mused. Maybe someday, ethical, upright, honest people would be elected to govern the United States. Joni had always been a dreamer. Joni also heard on the news that the Paris Peace Accords had been signed a few days earlier and the United States involvement in the Vietnam War would be over. That made Joni shake her shoulders. Would more soldiers be coming home and be like Pilot, a veteran of the Vietnam War and one of her lovers from last year who was either a government agent or a really dumb drug dealer?

Joni wasn't ready to see Pilot or anyone like him again and wished the best for all the other soldiers returning from Vietnam.

. . . .

"Do you always have to listen to the news, Joni? I much prefer KDKB and listening to music while we drive home." Gina had been riding to and from work with Joni since her car had been stolen.

"There's just so much going on in the world, Gina. I need to keep up."

"Okay, *fine.* It's been ten days, Joni. We need to go back to the police station and report the theft of my car." Joni headed that way.

This time they were dressed in their work clothing, and definitely not drunk. After reporting the theft and situation to the policeman who sat at the front desk, the girls waited to hear what to do.

"*Ten days?*" the policeman said. "That car is in Mexico by now. But I will give you a police report so you can report this to your insurance company."

With the police report in hand, the girls went out to Joni's truck. "Does that make any sense?" Gina said. "The other cop said to wait ten days, which we did, and this one says the car is probably in Mexico now. What are we going to do?"

"You," Joni said, "are going to file the police report with your insurance company and then we'll see about getting you another car when they pay up."

The girls went back to the apartment. Space Dog was waiting for them there.

"Gina, you know we are going to have to duck around your mother. She hates my truck being parked in front of her house and we don't want her to know about Pucci being stolen."

"Of course, Joni. I'll just keep thinking of things to tell her with excuses why we can't go visit. Right now I just want to go to bed and read magazines. You can make me a drink."

CHAPTER 14

Wednesday, January 31. President Nixon announced that he was sending Henry A. Kissinger to Hanoi for a three-day effort to make the peace more secure and lay the groundwork for reconstruction of Southeast Asia.

• •

JONI PULLED INTO THE ALLEY beside The Hut and parked by the empty lot next to it. She hadn't taken Gina to work today as Gina's company had scheduled a photo shoot about Gina being the 1972 Customer Service Rep of the Year. Gina took a taxi to the photo shoot and was getting another one back to The Hut when the picture shoot was over. Joni was a bit jealous as Gina's company had even paid for Gina to get her hair done for the photo shoot because the picture was going to be in the company's next newsletter with an article about Gina being the 1972 Customer Service Rep of the Year. Joni needed to get her hair cut, too, but that would have to wait until after she had enough money to pay the rent. Space Dog had opted to spend the day in the apartment.

Walking in the back door of The Hut and after a quick stop at the ladies' room, Joni saw that there were a lot of people there who had been at the Peckerwood party. Bob and Jill sat at the end of the bar with two empty stools next to them. Perfect for Gina and me, Joni thought, walking over and plopping down next to Jill. Joni noticed Max standing over in the corner drinking his beer alone. Gina would be happy to see him there.

"What's the word, bird?" she said to Jill, then to Florina, "A pitcher of beer, two glasses, and three coasters, please."

Florina smiled and walked to the center of the bar to get the pitcher and the glasses, knowing that if Joni was there, Gina would soon follow. No one at The Hut knew about Pucci being stolen so Gina arriving later than Joni was not unusual as the girls often used to take both cars to work.

"Here you go, Joni," Florina said. "And here's your coasters."

Joni picked up the pitcher and filled one glass, setting it on one coaster and putting the spare one next to it. She was reaching into her purse for a pen when Jill said, "We were just talking about going down to Rocky Point. We have a cottage down there and we're just deciding when we want to head on out."

"Rocky Point?" Joni said. "What's that?"

"Not a 'what' but a 'where,'" Bob said. "Puerto Peñasco. It's in Mexico, about sixty miles south of the

Arizona border, right on the water. People call it 'Arizona's Ocean' because it's the closest beach."

"Yeah," Jill continued, "and you can get the best shrimp there. We usually pick up a cooler or two to bring home to sell, and that pays for our gas and beer."

"Wow," Joni said. "Sounds like a great time."

"You oughta go down there. Lots of cheap little hotels to stay in. And, Vince and Bernice own a bar there, too. Not as nice as The Hut, but it's pretty good for Mexico."

Hmmm, Joni thought. The Hut wasn't a four-star establishment and maybe not even a two-star, but this was starting to sound like an adventure, no matter what the bar was like in Mexico.

"Let me run it by Gina and maybe we'll join you if it's over a weekend and we're not working."

"One good thing about being a substitute teacher," Bob said. "Work when you want to. Don't when you don't."

"One good thing about being a housewife," Jill added. "I can go anywhere anytime!"

Joni nodded but thought that she would rather work than be tied down to one man. She reached down to get her beer, looking to the front door just as Gina was walking in. With a *giant* bouffant hairdo. Gina had thick hair anyway, and the hairdresser had apparently taken advantage of that. Gina was smiling and nudging the boys as she walked the length of the bar. Joni set her glass on the bar, picked up the empty one, and poured Gina a beer, holding out the glass as Gina sat down next to her.

"What in the world did they do to your hair? It's *huge!*" Joni exclaimed.

"Yep," Bob said, leaning around Jill. "I heard they had big hair in Texas, but I've never seen anything like that before."

Gina tipped her head to the side, then sat up straight. "The bigger the hair, the closer to God," she said loudly in her best Texas accent, smiling, then adding, "Praise the Lord!"

"Praise the Lord!" repeated all those in The Hut who had heard Gina, raising their glasses and bottles in a toast, laughing and cheers sounding throughout the bar.

"So, how'd the shoot go?" Joni asked.

"Bang, bang," Gina said, smiling. "They asked me how I enjoyed the trip I won as Customer Service Rep of 1972, and I told them we had a delightful trip to a tropical paradise. I thought I'd leave out the part about the drug dealers, and the Federales, and especially the turista we picked up."

Jill broke in. "Turista? Where'd you go?"

"To Mazatlán," Gina and Joni said together. "What a trip that was," Gina continued. "We thought the price of drinks in the bars was too high so we bought a bottle of tequila and some orange juice. Which was reconstituted with Mexican water. Talk about turista. We had it bad."

"Well, Gina, Jill and Bob have invited us to go to Mexico again, to Rocky Point. Vince and Bernice have a bar there and there's great shrimp and we can stay in a little hotel and drink beer and..."

"Slow down, Joni. You'd better believe I'm drinking nothing but beer in Mexico from now on," Gina said, downing her glass.

"Gina, you don't drink anything but beer here," Joni said, elbowing her friend in the arm. Joni was glad that despite the car theft, Gina was starting to act like her old self again.

"And who's talking?" Gina replied. Jill and Bob laughed.

Then Bob said, "You girls really should come down for a weekend. Like we told Joni, cheap hotels, the bar, and something I've heard you girls might like—lots of boys. And Joni, I know you drive that red pickup truck with the camper shell on the back. Vince is looking for a way to smuggle a pool table down to his bar. The back of your truck just might be the way to do that."

"*Smuggle?*" Joni said, almost choking on her beer. "What are you talking about?"

"Vince doesn't want to pay the import fees to get the pool table down there. Worst that would happen if you got caught is that he'd have to pay the fees and a fine."

"We'll think about it," Gina said, Joni almost choking again on the "we." But she knew they would talk about it later.

Part Two

FEBRUARY 1973

When you're drinking and you're dreaming
There is nothing that can stop you
Got your plans, done your scheming
There'll be no one 'round to stop you
Whether legal or immoral, fattening, damnin' or untrue
Doesn't matter when we're singing our songs

—Joni's Songbook

CHAPTER 15

Friday, February 2. North Vietnam's government provided the names of only 7 of the 319 Americans who had been listed by the US as having been captured in Laos. There were 308 US servicemen and 4 civilians who had been listed as missing in action or as prisoners of war. President Richard Nixon sent his written State of the Union message to Congress rather than speaking to a joint session. For the first time since 1956, when Dwight D. Eisenhower was recovering from a heart attack, the president of the United States had the text printed rather than speaking on national television.

. . . .

JONI TOLD HER TEMP AGENCY that she wouldn't be working today and maybe not Monday. She had decided to take the pool table to Rocky Point. Gina was going to go down after work with Bob and Jill and would meet Joni there at Vince's bar. Gina really didn't want to deal with anything that might happen with the pool table hidden in the back of Joni's pickup truck, but she didn't tell that to Joni.

Early afternoon, Joni backed her truck up close to the rear door of The Hut, all the guys waving their arms and hands thinking Joni didn't know what she was doing and trying to direct her. Other than backing Pilot's Celica into a light pole at The Library bar last year, she was a pretty good backer-upper. Or so she thought.

"*Whoa*," Vince shouted, pulling Joni from her reflections. "We gotta have room to pop the top of the camper and pull the tailgate down."

Vince and Joe Ravioli lugged the top of the pool table out of the bar, muttering under their breath about how heavy this hunk of slate was. Even though it was a bar-sized pool table with only one piece of slate, the top weighed about four hundred pounds. The boys put one end of the tabletop on the tailgate of Joni's truck and pushed it into the camper. Pete Groat came out with the pool cues and cue stick rack and Boyer with the pool table legs.

Vince went to his van to retrieve a heavy blanket. "You gotta keep this covered, Joni. And keep the border agents occupied so they don't do more than glance in the back of the truck. Maybe you need to get a blouse that is lower cut."

For a flashing moment, Joni wondered what she was really doing, helping Vince get his pool table to Rocky Point, but that thought quickly passed. What the hey, she said to herself, let's get this adventure started.

Vince put a quilted furniture pad over the blanket on the pool table, hoping any border agent who looked into the truck would just think it was carpeting in the camper shell. Next, he put the tailgate into place and pulled down the camper top. Then he patted Joni's butt and said, "Happy trails, see you in Rocky Point."

Joni left The Hut and headed across Phoenix to the city of Buckeye where she turned left onto Highway 80 heading south. Yes, Joni thought, I did stop at the ladies' room at The Hut before I left, but I need to go again. Fortunately, Gila Bend was only about thirty miles from Buckeye and Joni knew she could wait until she got there.

Right after Joni saw the signs for the airport at Gila Bend, she saw signs for a truck stop. Aha, she thought, Just what I need. I can fill up my gas tank, get a drink, and use the facilities. She knew that Gina would have been complaining at her for stopping so soon, but Gina wasn't in the truck today.

Joni got off at the exit and pulled into the truck stop. She saw a parking space that looked perfect and turned abruptly into it.

"Doo-doo," Joni said out loud, feeling the load shift in the back of her truck and hoping everything was okay, as she did not want to piss off Vince. She walked around to the back of her pickup, opened the camper top door, and saw no damage other than a small dent in her left wheel cover, then shrugged, closed the camper door, and set the lock.

As she walked around the pickup to head for the store in the truck stop where she assumed the bathrooms would be, she saw a Phil Fancy's Fruits &

Vegetables truck pulling into the truck stop and heading to the back where the big rigs parked. Hmmm, that's the company that Wheeler drives for, she thought. Wouldn't it be a hoot if that was him! Then she hurried into the truck stop to pee.

Joni easily found the ladies' room. Afterward, she decided to stretch her legs and wander around the truck stop. Whoa, she thought, This place is full of men! She turned into the aisle where the CB radios were exhibited, and there was Wheeler.

"What are you doing here?" she asked as coyly as she could. Joni was not very coy in most people's minds, just direct.

"*Joni!* So good to see you. What are *you* doing here?" he said, reaching out and taking Joni into a warm hug.

"I'm on a secret mission," she mumbled, smothered into his shoulder.

"What? There are no secrets between us, right?"

Hmmm, Joni thought, Who knows? Then she answered, "You can't tell, but I'm taking a pool table to a bar in Rocky Point that is owned by the same people who own The Hut. Vince doesn't want to pay taxes on it so it is hidden in the back of the camper on my truck."

Wheeler started to laugh and couldn't stop. "Well," he said, "I know this is the real story because who could make that up. And where's Gina?"

"Gina is riding down with some of our friends. I'm meeting her there tonight. They're coming down after work."

"Well, my lady, let's have lunch together here. I have a bit of time before I can drive again on my logbook, so I have a few hours to waste. But of course, now that you are here, they won't be wasted!"

Joni thought about it and looked at her watch, knowing that she wasn't really good at night driving and she needed to get going. "Wheeler, as much as I'd like to have lunch with you, I really don't have a lot of time and I need to get back on the road. I'm not sure when the border closes at Lukeville and I have to get across today."

Wheeler just smiled. "Okay, little lady, I have a better idea. Let me show you my etchings in my truck."

Joni shrugged and said, "Okay. I didn't know that big rigs had etchings in them."

"It's a joke, Joni. Like men say when they want to get you into their bedroom. Let me show you my etchings..."

"Aha," Joni said, smiling big herself. "Let's go see the etchings."

Joni had never been in the sleeper of a big rig before. She used the handles on the side of the truck cab to pull herself up the steps into the front of the truck. She didn't need to worry because Wheeler assisted by pushing her butt up the stairs. What was it? she thought. Vince patted my butt... Wheeler is pushing my butt...

Once inside, Wheeler joined her and gestured to the back. "The etchings, my dear, are in there," he said, pulling aside the privacy curtain that hung between the front of the cab where he drove and the back where he slept. Joni laughed again, then proceeded to the back of the cab. Wheeler turned on a radio with soft music, and the next hour passed in a flurry of lovemaking.

"I gotta go now," Joni said, pulling on her shirt and pants.

"I know, but I'm sure glad we got to see each other. And Joni, if you are going to Rocky Point, you need to get on the big highway and then take the exit for Highway 85. It goes all the way to the border."

"Well, thanks for that info. I'd probably end up lost," Joni said. "But pretty amazing, huh? That we find each other at a truck stop in the middle of the desert!"

"Nothing would have made me happier than finding you today, Joni. I know I said this before, but I'll catch you on the flip-flop." This time Joni knew what he meant.

After another stop at the ladies' room in the truck stop, Joni took Wheeler's directions and found Highway 85 heading south. The signs said that Lukeville was only eighty-five miles from Gila Bend, and Joni was pretty sure she could make it there without another bathroom stop.

As she neared Lukeville, Joni started getting nervous. After all, she had a pool table in the back of her truck that she didn't want to talk about. Deep breaths, she thought. You have to do this. In and out, in and out—then she thought about Wheeler—in and out, in and out.

There were about eight cars in front of Joni's truck at the border. When it was her turn, the border agent just asked, "Where are you going?"

"Rocky Point," Joni answered.

"And what is your business there?" the agent asked again.

"Business? I'm going for fun. I hear that the shrimp are the best there, the ocean is clear, and the bars are full of men. That's what I'm going for!" Her best lines, practiced more than once before she hit the border.

"Okay, you look like you want to have fun, so I'm letting you through. Anything to declare?"

"Declare? What does that mean?"

"Declare. Anything you are taking into Mexico that needs to be declared?"

Joni gulped, tilted her head to the side like Gina did, wished she had Gina's dimples, and said, "No, sir, just my luggage and my bathing suit."

The agent hesitated, looked at the truck, then waved Joni on. "Free to cross the border," he said.

Joni finally let out the breath she had been holding and followed the signs to Rocky Point. It was sixty-five miles, and she was going to get there as soon as possible.

The directions Vince gave to Joni on how to find his bar were to enter the town, take a right at the Catholic church, and just follow the street until she saw the bar on the right side of the street facing the ocean with Ballena Hill on the left. This was Old Town in Puerto Peñasco, where the original town had been built. Joni found it difficult to pay attention to the street because the town was so unique and quaint, and quickly found La Cabaña, Vince's bar in Mexico. As she pulled up to the bar, Gina, Bob, and Jill came running out the front door to her truck.

"How did you get here before I did?" Joni asked, confused because she thought they were driving down after work.

"Surprise, Joni! I took the day off. Bob didn't have a teaching assignment, and Jill was ready to go. How did we miss you on the road?" Gina said.

"Well, I may have had a slight layover at the truck stop in Gila Bend," Joni responded, shrugging her shoulders and blushing slightly. "I ran into Wheeler at the truck stop." Gina shook her head as Joni continued. "Not literally. He was just there and wanted to show me his etchings and somehow we ended up in his truck and I spent an hour or so there."

"Who's Wheeler?" Jill asked.

Gina stepped in. "He's Joni's trucker boyfriend. Tall and handsome and only around sometimes so it works out well for everyone."

"Hey, I really like him," Joni said, defending herself.

"Yeah, yeah, but you really like Tom Dixon, too," Gina continued. The girls were having a discussion as if no one else were around.

At that point, Vince came out of the bar with four locals. "How did you do at the border?" he asked Joni.

"No problem. They didn't even look in the camper, just asked me where I was going and I told them I was meeting friends in Rocky Point."

"Good job, Joni. I have some men coming out to help unload the pool table. Why don't you and your friends go inside and I'll buy you all a beer."

The men Vince had hired appeared from the side of the bar and started to unload the pool table. They were having much less trouble doing that than when the pool table was loaded into Joni's pickup back in Tempe. Everyone headed inside for a beer.

"Hey, Gina," Joni shouted over the noise in the bar. "Once they have the pool table out of my camper we can sleep there."

"Joni, Joni, Joni. Didn't you see what's over La Cabaña? There are small hotel rooms up there. I already rented one of them for us. Just a slight inconvenience, well, more for you, because the bathrooms are out back so we have to walk down the stairs to use them."

"Hmmmph," Joni said, scowling, then she cheered up. "Okay, I'll deal with it. At least we are here and we can par-teee and not have to drive home!"

The girls joined their friends at a table in the bar, and the evening began with bottles of beer and shots of tequila. After the long drive for everyone, it was an early evening and they all went upstairs to their rooms. Joni of course stopped at the downstairs bathroom, which to her looked a lot like an outhouse, before going to her room.

CHAPTER 16

Saturday, February 3. The Vietnam peace agreement provided that the US allocate about $500 million a year in military aid to Laos and Cambodia. Despite that, Kissinger urged the White House to continue the military aid and not to withdraw any US military personnel from these two countries.

. . . .

JONI WOKE FIRST, WALKED DOWNSTAIRS to go to the bathroom, then back to the room to wait for Gina to get up. She quietly hummed a bit of "Your Sweet and Shiny Eyes" by Bonnie Raitt, set in Laredo. Joni thought that Puerto Peñasco was her own little Mexican paradise.

"Wake up, Gina," Joni said when she couldn't stand it any longer. Gina rolled over, squinted at Joni, and said, "What's the hurry? We have all day here."

Joni shrugged. "Well, I'm hungry."

"Yeah, me too, so let's get this party going."

Walking downstairs, the girls noticed that the bar was open and wonderful smells were emanating from it.

"Come on, Joni, let's check it out."

Joni opened the door for Gina and was surprised to see the bar was full and people were eating breakfast.

"I didn't know the bar served food," Gina said. "Oh look, Bob and Jill are already here."

"Come on over and sit with us," Jill said, motioning to the girls. "You gotta try the huevos rancheros, they are really great."

Joni looked at Jill's plate, saying, "Looks like fried eggs floating in a lot of tomato sauce to me."

Everyone except Gina who had heard Joni's comment was laughing.

"Well, Joni," Bob said, "that's basically what it is—a tortilla with salsa and a fried egg on top. Give it a try."

"Okay," Joni responded while Gina nodded her head. "Can't dance."

Both girls ordered the huevos rancheros and decided that a Bloody Mary would just be the perfect way to start the day. Despite Joni's original assessment of the breakfast dish, both girls enjoyed it and decided they would order it again.

"So what's up today?" Gina asked Jill. "I had hoped to do some shopping."

"No problem," Jill responded. "There is a great local flea market within walking distance of the bar and they have lot of local artists showing their wares. See these?" she said, pointing to her earrings. "I got them at the flea market last time we were down. I love the Mexican silver."

"Hurry up, Joni, finish those eggs swimming in salsa," Gina said, punching Joni in the arm. "I'm ready to spend some money!"

Joni finished her eggs quickly. "I'm going to the bathroom first, Gina," she said, then ran out the back door of the bar. She returned shortly and said, "Well, what are you waiting for?"

Gina just laughed.

The girls walked a few blocks and heard some mariachi music. Walking a bit faster, they soon came upon the flea market.

"This is wonderful," Gina said. "Look at all the vendors. Look at the jewelry. Look at the shells. We can spend half of the day here. And look, there is even a vendor selling bottles of beer. I think I'm ready to get started." She walked over to the beer vendor.

Great, thought Joni. Lots of beer and no bathrooms. At least it wasn't too far back to the bar.

After a few hours, the girls were tired and Gina had spent her travel money. She had a new pair of silver earrings, a pair of shell earrings, a serape she planned to put on the sofa at the apartment, a Mexican embroidered blouse, and a small stuffed donkey to go on the coffee table at the apartment. Joni bought only beer because she wanted to save her money for the rent that was coming due. But she was already planning to ask to wear Gina's new blouse at some point.

"Why did you buy the stuffed donkey?" Joni asked.

"Joni, it's good luck to see a donkey. I am going to put the donkey on our coffee table right by the goat chess game and we can look at him every day. Just think about our luck!"

"Uh, okay. Do we have to pet it or anything?"

Gina looked at her, eyes wide open, and said, "Really, Joni? It's a stuffed animal." Then she smiled and said, "Actually it's said that petting a donkey will bring you prosperity. We can always use that."

Joni said, "Okay, let's get another beer and go back to our room."

"Our room for a minute, but the bar as soon as possible!"

Back at the bar, the girls planned to go upstairs to stow Gina's goodies. Joni stopped first at the bathroom. Gina just shook her head.

"You just shouldn't drink beer when we are not near a bathroom," Gina said as she walked up the stairs to their room. Joni hurried and joined Gina.

"So, what do we do now?" Joni asked Gina.

"I think we take a nap and then we go down to the bar and just have us an evening. All the guys are out fishing, but they should be back in a few hours. Let's see what we can find to do there tonight."

A nap it was. For the second time that day, Joni woke first, then shook Gina, saying, "Wake up, Gina. Time to par-teee."

Gina put on her new blouse and her new silver earrings and looked at Joni. "Well, what are you going to wear?"

"Uh, do you have anything I can borrow in your suitcase?"

Gina had anticipated this. She turned and opened her suitcase and threw a black tank top at Joni. "Just put this on. Add one of your scarves around your neck. And whatever earrings you have that are long and dangly."

Joni shrugged, catching the black top. Fortunately, she had a few scarves in her suitcase and chose a turquoise one to add color. "If I could borrow your turquoise earrings that would be perfect."

Gina shook her head again. "Joni, you need to make more money and buy some things for yourself." She handed her turquoise earrings to Joni. "And don't lose them," Gina admonished.

Downstairs again. The bar was full by this time. Bob and Jill looked like they had been there all day, but Gina didn't ask. Jill could get testy at times. The girls joined the couple at the bar and ordered beer for the group. The evening began.

"So, Jill," Gina said, "we want to take some shrimp back with us like you and Bob do. Where's the best place to get some? Joni has a cooler in the back of her truck."

Jill looked at Bob and then said, "Well... and Bob, let me know if you agree... you can pick up shrimp at basically any of the vendors on the road out of town. Usually the shrimp are fresh. But you need to be careful where you get your ice. I'd suggest buying it here at the bar. Otherwise, you are going to get ice from Mexican water and you told us what happened to you last time you went to Mexico." The girls started laughing.

Bob was laughing along with everyone else. "I agree," he said. "Jill is right. Just come on down to the bar in the morning and fill your cooler with bar ice, then pick up the shrimp somewhere down the road."

"Lord knows I don't want turista again," Gina said, sticking her fingers in her dimples, then motioning to the bartender to bring the four of them a shot of tequila. "It's been a great time down here. Thanks for telling us about it."

Vince walked over to the group and said to Joni, "And thanks to you for getting the pool table here. You can see what a hit it has already become." He pointed to the pool table with stacks of quarters on it, then told the bartender that the shots of tequila were on the house.

A few hours and a few more shots of tequila later, the girls said goodbye to everyone, letting them know they were going back to Tempe in the morning. Joni headed for the outside bathroom, then soon joined Gina in their room. It was time to sleep.

CHAPTER 17

Sunday, February 4. The US television news show *60 Minutes* aired a segment, "The Selling of Colonel Herbert," that led to the CBS network being sued for libel by US Army Lieutenant Colonel Anthony Herbert. The lawsuit would lead to a landmark US Supreme Court decision in 1979 in *Herbert v. Lando*, which rejected a claim of First Amendment protection against discovery requests of the editorial process. Herbert would end up losing his lawsuit in 1986. Herbert was best known for his claims that he witnessed war crimes in Vietnam, which his commanding officer refused to investigate.

· · · · · · · · · · · · · · · · · · · ·

JONI WOKE EARLY, RUNNING DOWNSTAIRS to the bathroom. Upon her return, she woke Gina, saying, "We gotta get going. I want to make it back to the apartment while it is still cool outside so the shrimp are okay."

Gina grunted. "How many tequilas do you think we had last night?"

"Cumulatively I think about a hundred! But really, I don't think either of us had more than four or five."

"And a couple of beers. At least we didn't get turista this time."

"I agree and I don't want to get it, so let's pack up and then stop at the bar to fill the cooler with ice. Maybe have more huevos rancheros if you're hungry."

Gina moved her head from side to side and shrugged her shoulders. "You know what, Joni. I'd rather wait until we get farther up the road and have a McDonald's cheeseburger for breakfast. It will soak up the alcohol in our systems."

The girls hurried to pack and carried everything down to Joni's truck. Joni got out the cooler and told Gina that she would go get the ice from the bar. Shortly after that they were on the road back to Tempe.

"Hey, Joni, let's don't stop at the first vendor for shrimp we see. I feel like that one might not be the freshest."

Joni never argued with Gina's "logic," even if she thought differently.

"Okay, how about the second one?"

"Yes, I think that's the one for us."

Joni was barely on the outskirts of town when she passed the first shrimp vendor. A short drive after that she saw the second vendor.

"That's it, Joni. Just pull on over."

Joni got the cooler out of the back of the truck as Gina went to negotiate with the vendor. Gina thought she could speak Spanish by adding an "o" to the back of every word. Fortunately, this vendor spoke a bit of English.

The girls bought four pounds of shrimp to take home and put it in the cooler. Joni carried the cooler back to her truck. The girls continued north on Highway 85.

"Where's a McDonald's?" Gina asked. "I'm starving."

"I don't really recall seeing one on the way down. When we get to Gila Bend, we can stop at the truck stop where I ran into Wheeler. They have food inside and we can get some to go. Don't want to let the shrimp stay too long in the cooler."

Gila Bend was only about a half hour away at this point.

"I'm really starving, Joni," Gina grouched.

"It's right up the road, Gina. Plus, they have really nice bathrooms."

"We're eating first, Joni. You can just wait. And maybe we'll eat inside the truck stop so you don't spill anything on you while you drive."

Joni was used to Gina's gritching so just continued to drive. It wasn't long until she pulled into the truck stop. Locking up the camper door on the back of her truck so no one could steal the shrimp, Joni said, "Come on, Gina. Let's get something to eat. You'll feel much better then."

Gina agreed, and the girls went inside. The burgers were excellent, the iced tea good but of course not as good as Texas "sweet tea" per Gina. Gina only complained once but drank it all nonetheless. After a quick bathroom stop for Joni, the girls were back on the road.

"How much longer, Joni?"

"Not much. We'll be home soon. What are we going to do with all that shrimp?"

Gina smiled and raised her eyebrows. "Joni, we're going boy fishing!"

"What?"

"Stop by The Hut before we go home, and we'll invite all the guys over to have some shrimp we just picked up in Mexico. They'll go nuts, of course, and we can have a great party."

"Okay, but what about Benson?"

"Benson? We'll find him tomorrow. This is the last day of my weekend vacation and I'm going to enjoy it. Ain't no crime."

Joni just continued driving. It wasn't too long before they reached Buckeye and were traveling across Phoenix over to Tempe. Joni tuned onto Second Street and parked behind The Hut.

"What now?" she asked Gina.

"We go inside, order two cold beers, then tell everyone we like there that we are having a shrimp boil at our apartment. They can bring the beer and we'll provide the shrimp."

"Well, okay. What if people show up we don't like?"

"They won't. People we like already know where we live. And people we don't like, they don't know where we live. Not to worry, Joni. Not to worry."

"Okay, let's go in and get this party going."

The girls walked in the back door to the sound of people cheering. Football was over for the year, so the television set in The Hut was not on. Everyone was gathered around the pool table. Florina was tending bar that day.

"What's going on," Gina asked Florina.

"We're having a pool tournament and it looks like Boyer just won it. The prize is twenty dollars plus two pitchers of free beer. Caffy has been his cheerleader and she stirred up the crowd to cheer him on. Ready for a pitcher today?"

"No thanks," Gina replied. "Just one glass of beer for each of us. We've been in Puerto Peñasco and brought home a lot of shrimp. We're here to find people to come over and party."

"I don't get off until six o'clock, but I'll be over when my shift is over."

"Cool beans." Florina went to get the girls' beer. Joni went to the ladies' room. Gina got the stools at the bar for her and Joni.

Once the cheering stopped, everyone went back to drinking beer.

"Hey," Joe Ravioli shouted. "Gina and Joni are back from Mexico!"

With that notice, all of the girls' friends stopped by to say hello and welcome them back.

"Okay, okay," Gina said, putting her hands in the air and stopping the shouting. "Joni and I brought back four pounds of fresh shrimp and we are taking them home right now for a party. We're having a shrimp boil. Everyone is welcome. Each of you should bring a six-pack or some other delight. Be there or be square."

Joe Ravioli, Boyer, Craig from Colorado, Boston Jack, and Leroy B. all shouted that they would be there shortly. Gina and Joni finished their glasses of beer and left to go boil the shrimp.

"Do you think this is the right thing to do?" Joni asked Gina when they were back in Joni's truck.

"It's the only thing to do, silly girl. We have to go to work tomorrow, so let's make the best of the day. You *do* have a job tomorrow, right?"

"Probably not. I told them I was taking off Friday and maybe Monday because I wasn't sure how long we would be gone, but I'll call them and be sure I have something on Tuesday. Yeah, yeah, I know . . . the rent money."

Back at the Windbell, the girls quickly unloaded the truck and took everything up to their apartment. Gina dumped her suitcase in her room and ran to the kitchen, pulling out the largest pans the girls had.

"Joni, come here and fill all our pans with water and get them on the stove."

Joni had started to unpack her suitcase, but stopped and went right to the kitchen. "You think we can cook four pounds of shrimp?"

"Sure, no problem."

Gina was looking intently through the kitchen cabinet that held her spices. Joni rarely cooked so knew nothing about that.

"Aha," Gina said, pulling out a can of seasoning. "Zatarain's Shrimp and Crab Boil. Oh boy, we're going to smell just like New Orleans."

Joni started filling the pans with water and put them on the four burners to start boiling. "Uh, Gina, I don't think all the shrimp are going to fit into these four pans."

"Not to worry, worry wart. The shrimp don't take long to cook and they have to cool before we can eat them, so we'll just take the done shrimp and put them here on the counter." Gina pointed to the other side of the kitchen. "I'll go get the newspaper we have saved from your job hunting and we'll put them on that. Very New Orleans."

While Joni was putting the shrimp into the boiling water, Gina went into her bedroom and pulled the stuffed donkey from her suitcase, taking it and putting it prominently on the living room coffee table.

"There," she said. "One donkey just waiting to be seen. You'd better look at it every day so we continue to have good luck."

Joni just shook her head and said, "Sure, good luck. Just what we need."

It didn't take very long to get all the shrimp cooked and onto the newspaper to cool. Joni pulled out the paper plates and lots of paper napkins and set them on the counter next to the shrimp.

"Gina, what are we going to do for shrimp sauce?"

Gina thought for a moment. "Oh, yikes, I forgot about that. I'll be back in a moment." She rushed out the door and ran downstairs, knocking on Rudy's apartment door.

"Gina," he said, "what in the world do you want now?"

"Shrimp sauce. Do you have any shrimp sauce?"

Rudy laughed. "Shrimp sauce? What every young single guy has in his kitchen. You are too funny."

"Well," Gina said, turning her head to the side and showing her dimples, "we just brought home four pounds of fresh shrimp from Mexico and we're cooking them for a party. If you and whoever is here now want to join us, get thyself to the store and bring us four jars of shrimp cocktail sauce. The others are bringing the beer."

"Who could say no to you, Gina?" Rudy laughed and closed the door. Gina returned to her apartment, telling Joni that everything was under control. Just then the boys from The Hut starting appearing. As ever, the door to the girls' apartment was open. Boyer came first and as expected, Caffy was with him. Oh well, thought Gina, How much trouble can she be?

The others followed, bringing in beer and a bottle of wine and a bottle of tequila that Gina quickly put in the refrigerator.

"Help yourself," Gina said as she closed the refrigerator door, pulling out the shot glasses for anyone who wanted tequila as well as beer.

Soon the apartment was rocking with the album sounds of KDKB. Joni picked up her plastic shot glass and filled it with tequila.

"A to-kill-ya for the troops," Joni said, laughing and downing the tequila. She shook her head and then decided that it was too early for this, instead opening a beer to drink. Or maybe I need a glass of wine, she thought, downing the beer first.

Rudy finally showed up with the shrimp cocktail sauce, and Gina pronounced that it was time to eat. Everyone rushed to the kitchen and began filling their plates with freshly boiled shrimp. The conversation overshadowed the radio, and smiles were abundant. Only Caffy seemed not to be having fun. She sat on a chair at the gateleg table and ate only a few shrimp. After lunch, Boyer was in the living room playing goat chess with Joe Ravioli.

"Hey, Gina," Joe Ravioli said. "What's with the stuffed donkey on the coffee table?"

Gina smiled. "Well, don't you know that seeing a donkey is good luck. And, if you pet the donkey's back, it is not only good luck but also prosperity." She slugged back a drink of her beer.

Everyone rushed to the coffee table to pet the donkey's back. At this stage in the party, no one remembered that the coffee table rested on only three legs, that the fourth had broken up a long time ago and was only propped under the table. Shortly after that, the table toppled onto the floor, flinging the stuffed donkey onto the carpet and throwing the metal goat on the goat chess board under the television console.

"Oops," someone said.

"Not to worry," Gina shouted over the noise. "The donkey is just fine. The goat is just fine. No one had a drink on the table so no mess, no fuss. I say just pick up the table, put the fourth leg under it, and get back to your goat chess game. Maybe we should put the donkey on the gateleg table so everyone can pet it. Good luck. Fortune. What we all need."

Boyer stood up. "Beer is what we all need. And tequila! Who wants what?" Boyer fixed drinks for everyone. The party was going on longer than the girls thought it would, and at some point, Gina retired to her bedroom. She had to work tomorrow. Before closing her bedroom door, she turned to Joni and said, "Guess who's cleaning up tomorrow? And then find something from your agency so you can work on Tuesday."

Joni frowned.

"But Joni, it's okay. This is one of the most wonderful weekends we have ever had. Who would have thunk it?"

Joni smiled and said, "Good night, Gina. I'll take care of everything."

Forever friends, Joni thought. Forever friends.

CHAPTER 18

Monday, February 5. Services were held at Arlington National Cemetery for Army Lieutenant Colonel William B. Nolde, the last American soldier killed before the Vietnam ceasefire.

. . . .

JONI HEARD GINA'S ALARM CLOCK go off and walked over to turn on the snooze alarm, then went into the kitchen to heat water for Gina's coffee.

Oh boy, Joni thought, looks like we had a huge party here last night. It will take me half of the day to get this back in order. Then she poured water into the coffee cup with instant Kava, adding milk and sugar, and carrying it into Gina's bedroom.

"Wake up, wake up for Jesus, ye soldiers of the cross," Joni sang to Gina to the tune of "Stand Up, Stand Up for Jesus," one of Joni's mother's favorite hymns.

"Joni, must you always be so happy in the mornings? Give me my coffee and let me get ready for work. And you, my dear, better find some work yourself for tomorrow."

"I'll call them as soon as I drop you off at your office. I'm sure they will have something for me to do starting tomorrow. Today you may recall I am cleaning the kitchen. Who knew that so few men could make such a mess in that short a time?"

"Well, it would have been better if Caffy had helped, but she just sat like a lump at the gateleg table and looked like she was too good even to be peeling the shrimp," Gina said as she sipped her coffee.

"At least Boyer took her home with him, so I didn't have to deal with him yesterday. I really hope they stay together."

"And Joni, after you finish cleaning up and doing the laundry, get dressed for a night on the town. We're going to the Beef Rigger when you pick me up from work. Time to get back into the folk song thing."

Joni made a face. "You mean time to get back into Tom Dixon and Benson. Benson doesn't always show up on Mondays at the Beef Rigger."

Gina turned her head sideways. "Joni, I *know* Benson will be there tonight. I just feel it. All the way to my toes."

Joni gave up and went to get dressed, pulling on her wheat jeans and a T-shirt so she could take Gina to work.

Joni's day went by quickly. First she called her temp agency and learned that they had found her a job typing for the rest of the week. It was located out in Fountain Hills, so a lot of driving but at least it was a job. Then Joni tackled the kitchen, wondering how she could find a way to recycle all the shrimp shells from the party yesterday. She gave up and put them into the trash.

Late afternoon and Joni remembered they were going to see Tom Dixon after she picked up Gina from work. Joni had not had time to do the laundry so had to settle for one of the shirts that she didn't wear in Puerto Peñasco that was still in her suitcase. Okay, it was the brown one and it went fine with her wheat jeans and she couldn't remember if Tom Dixon had ever seen it.

"Joni, Joni," Gina said as she jumped into the cab of Joni's truck when Joni came to pick her up from work. "I'm so glad you are here. After such a lovely weekend, this day has been a drag. Take me to the Beef Rigger, wench."

Joni headed that way.

As they walked into the Beef Rigger, they heard Tom Dixon singing and, turning the corner into the bar area, saw that Benson was indeed there doing sound.

"Told you so," Gina smirked as she turned toward Joni and smiled.

The girls found a table in between the sound board and the stage, ordered their double John Collins drinks from the waitress, and waited for the set to end. When it did, Tom Dixon stopped to shake hands with a few of the other patrons there, then walked right up to Gina and Joni's table.

"Ah, to what do I owe this pleasure?" he asked.

Gina stuck her fingers in her dimples, tilted her head, and said, "To *our* pleasure, of course!"

Tom Dixon laughed as Benson turned on the canned music and came over to the girls' table, leaning over Gina and planting a kiss on her cheek.

"Sigh . . . I think I'm falling in love," Gina said, pretending to faint into Benson's arms.

Everyone laughed.

"So what's happening with you girls?" Tom Dixon asked.

Gina stepped up to answer. "We just returned from Puerto Peñasco down in Mexico. The same guy who owns The Hut has a bar down there with rooms for rent over the bar. Joni smuggled a pool table down there for Vince so we got a lot of free beer and tequila all weekend long."

"Wow, sounds like fun," Benson said. "I've heard a lot about Puerto Peñasco. Great place to buy shrimp."

"You bet, cowboy," Gina answered. "We brought home four pounds of fresh shrimp yesterday and cooked them up at the apartment. All gone today, so sorry that we weren't able to find you to invite you to the party."

Benson broke into a big smile. "We'll just have to find a way to remedy that, won't we?"

Gina smiled even bigger and nodded her head. Tom Dixon looked at Joni and shrugged his shoulders. He had already told Joni that he was married and knew she was okay with that.

"I've got to get back on the stage and play some more," Tom Dixon said. "Are you girls going to The Hut after here or are you going home?"

Gina answered. "We're going home. We'll meet you there!"

The girls each had another John Collins and got a plate from the buffet table. They listened to Tom Dixon sing "Paradise" by John Prine before they left.

It was almost nine before the boys got to the Windbell.

"A cup of coffee for me," Tom Dixon said to Joni. "I can't stay long and I have to get back home tonight. I hope you understand."

"Of course I do. Cream and sugar or black?" Joni asked, never having made Tom Dixon coffee before.

"How about black with a shot of brandy. I think you girls keep brandy on hand here."

"Yup, you betcha," Gina said. "For our famous Brandy Alexanders. We have our own recipe and use vanilla ice cream. Yum-yum."

"I'll take one," Benson said. "Sounds like the perfect drink in bed." He turned his head toward Gina's bedroom."

"Oh, Joni," Gina sang. "Would you please make me two Brandy Alexanders à la Gina and bring them to my bedroom. And remember to knock first!"

Joni just shook her head. "Of course."

After delivering the Brandy Alexanders to Gina and Benson, Joni returned to the gateleg table where Tom Dixon was drinking his coffee and brandy.

"So what's up, buttercup?" she said.

Tom Dixon put his coffee cup down on the gateleg table. "Joni, it's been really difficult for me at home. My wife is a terror. My children don't listen to me. They only believe what she says. I have to go out and sing and entertain people who don't want to hear about my problems. They don't even want to know about them. I'm just the person who sings happy songs to make people happy. You are the one thing in my life that is always the same. You and Gina make people feel good. And I don't mean just the sex."

"I'm so sorry," Joni replied. "It has to be terrible for you."

"At times, yes. Others, well, I deal with it. Are you okay? Because I really need to go home tonight."

Joni leaned over and gave Tom Dixon a kiss. "Yes, I'm just fine. Drive safely." She remembered her English studies and didn't say "Drive safe," then added, "I'll see you down the line."

Tom Dixon responded with another kiss, then patted Joni on the behind and walked out the door of the apartment.

So what's with everyone patting me on the behind? Joni asked herself as she closed and locked the front door to the apartment. She wasn't ready for anyone else to walk in tonight.

CHAPTER 19

Tuesday, February 6. Efforts to find a peaceful end to the Vietnam War were stalled when South Vietnam would not allow the Vietcong to meet with the International Control Commission at Can Tho, the largest city in the Mekong Delta region.

. . . .

JONI WAS UP EARLY AND out the door before Gina and Benson were awake as she had to drive all the way to Fountain Hills for her new job. Benson had already planned to drive Gina to work today, so Joni didn't have to do it. Joni left a note for Gina, letting her know that she would pick her up after work.

Gina was heating up water for coffee, and Benson was sitting at the gateleg table.

"Gina," Benson said, turning toward the kitchen where Gina was fixing their coffee. "It looks like I may need to be out of town for a few days. I'm scouting out new venues for craft fairs. Think you'll be okay without me?" He smiled his big smile.

"Well, big boy, I'm not sure about that but I'll make do as best I can," Gina said, showing her dimples.

"Great. It will probably be next week before I get back to town. I'll let you know as soon as my schedule is finalized." He took a sip from his coffee cup. "And are you about ready to go to work? Time is passing us by."

Gina scrunched up her face. "I don't want to go to work today."

"But you have to, little girl!"

Gina loved their bantering. She was feeling more and more like Benson could be her boyfriend.

Later that afternoon, Joni finished work and headed to downtown Phoenix to pick up Gina.

"Whaddya want to do today?" she asked as Gina opened the door to the pickup truck.

"I think we need a Hut night," Gina answered. Joni headed that way.

Joni parked her truck behind The Hut, and the girls entered through the back door. It seemed that a lot of people were there.

"What's going on, Florina?" Gina asked the bartender.

"It's Pete Groat's birthday today, and we're having a birthday party here for him. He should be here shortly."

Gina looked at Joni. "You know what we have to do, right?"

Joni nodded, looked at Florina, and said, "We'll be right back."

The girls hurried to Bashas' grocery store, parked, and walked to the deli section of the store.

"Let's get a chocolate cake," Gina said. Joni nodded her head.

The girls picked out a two-layer round chocolate cake, and when the deli lady asked if they wanted anything printed on it, the girls started giggling.

"No, thanks," Gina sputtered as she giggled, "we'll take care of it."

On the way to the checkout counter, the girls stopped at the candy aisle and picked out a large package of M&M's. After paying, they rushed to the parking lot. Joni opened the M&M's and started putting them randomly on the cake, pushing each one softly into the icing. Gina took a handful of M&M's and helped her do it.

"Perfect," Gina said when they had stuck all the M&M's into the cake. "Happy Birthday Pete Groat in Braille!"

Joni just smiled and stuck the two M&M's into her mouth that somehow she didn't get onto the cake.

"Cheater." Gina had caught her.

Back at The Hut, the girls once again parked behind The Hut and entered through the back door, Gina carefully carrying the cake. No way would she allow Joni to do that, klutz that Joni was.

By this time, Pete Groat was at The Hut and people were buying him beer. Gina walked up to Pete Groat, held out the cake, and said, "Happy birthday from me and Joni."

Pete Groat showed his surprise by choking on his glass of beer. Once he calmed down, he said, "Thanks, an M&M cake."

"No, Pete," Gina said. "It is a Happy Birthday Pete Groat cake written in Braille."

Everyone at The Hut laughed. Pete Groat smiled his biggest smile ever.

"You girls really know how to take care of a man! This is the best birthday cake I have ever had."

The party continued with beer and warm wishes and hugs all the way around. Gina and Joni left early to go home and get ready for the rest of the week.

CHAPTER 20

Thursday, February 9. Max Yasgur, owner of the Wood-stock festival farmland, died of a heart attack. He was fifty-three. In 1969 his dairy farm was the site of the Woodstock Music and Art Fair.

• • • • • • • • • • • • • • • • • • • •

AS USUAL, JONI PICKED UP Gina after work. Joni was excited and had something to tell Gina.

"Gina, Gina, guess what?"

"What, Joni?"

"Remember that biker bar over on Sixteenth Street in Phoenix called Ratz?"

"Not really, remind me."

Joni huffed, then straightened up as she didn't want to irritate Gina. "Burglar Bernie turned me on to it. It's a pretty rough place but okay overall."

"Not somewhere I would want to go," Gina said strongly.

"Well, maybe not. But tonight they want me to bring my guitar and sing my songs. Me, of all people."

"You'd better be careful. I know how much you love that guitar."

"Not to worry. The stage is about six feet higher than the bar area. You have to climb up on a ladder to get there and then the bouncer takes the ladder away so no one can get to you."

Gina laughed so hard she thought she would burst. "Joni, do you think *you* can climb up a ladder with your guitar? You can barely walk up a staircase."

"I'm going to do it, Gina. You told me that I needed to play my guitar more this year, so I'm doing it."

"Well, fine. Take me to The Hut and I'll find someone to get me home later. I can't wait to hear about this when you get back."

"I'm on at eight, so I should be home by ten."

Gina just shook her head. "Okay, Joni. This has to be one of your craziest ideas."

After dropping Gina at The Hut, Joni went home to change. And thought about it. Maybe it was a crazy idea. At least she would have her truck and could leave whenever she wanted to, given that the bouncer would put the ladder back up to the stage so she could get down.

Joni parked near Ratz and carried her guitar into the bar.

"Aha, there she is," the bartender shouted over the crowd's noise. "Our singer for the evening."

Joni blushed. "Uh, could I get a glass of water to have while I am singing?"

"Anything for you, honey," the bartender said, shoving a glass of water across the bar to Joni.

The bouncer came over to Joni. "I'll be helping you get up to the stage and carry your guitar up the ladder for you."

Joni sighed. She hadn't really thought this whole thing through.

In about fifteen minutes, Joni was on the elevated stage with her guitar in tune. She opened her set with a Hank Williams song, "I Saw the Light." It was a joke to her, fooling them into thinking she was a Christian singer. No one applauded. A few booed. Joni just smiled.

Then she burst into her own rendition of "Richland Woman Blues." She knew that would go over better. The song contained one of her favorite lines, about the rooster crowing and a woman out on the town without her husband knowing. Joni was right, the crowd loved it.

Joni sang a few of her own songs along with other country songs. She had decided to end with "Throwing Enchiladas at the Wall." She started singing.

> *Throwing enchiladas at the wall*
> *Throwing enchiladas at the wall*
> *We never understood why at all*
> *We were throwing enchiladas at the wall*

"More, more," the crowd shouted. Then one really large biker said, "Joni, sing 'Throwing Enchiladas at the Wall' again. I really love that song."

Apparently, everyone respected this man and started chanting, "Throwing Enchiladas at the Wall,

Throwing Enchiladas at the Wall." Joni picked up her guitar and started singing the song one more time.

A very small biker cringed and started moving toward the door. The others stood in front of him and blocked his way. Joni kept singing while watching this play out.

As Joni finished her song, the large biker picked up the smaller man and threw him against the wall. Everyone else laughed.

Joni thanked her audience and said good night, hoping that the bouncer would be there soon with the ladder so she could go home. As the bouncer was helping her get her guitar down from the stage, she asked him why the large man had thrown the smaller man at the wall.

"Easy. His nickname is Enchilada."

Joni forced a laugh, then quickly exited the bar with her guitar. She decided that she wasn't going to play there anymore.

CHAPTER 21

Saturday, February 10. The Pentagon announced the names of the American military prisoners of war in the first group scheduled to be released from Communist camps in North and South Vietnam, after notifying the prisoners' relatives. Of the 134 servicemen, 19 will be freed in South Vietnam and 115 in Hanoi. The list included the name of Lieutenant Commander Everett Alvarez of Santa Clara, California, the first pilot captured by the North Vietnamese. His plane was shot down on August 5, 1964. The State Department said it had received a list of 8 government civilian employees who would be among the first group of prisoners to be freed in South Vietnam.

The number one song was Elton John's "Crocodile Rock."

. . . .

GINA WAS LOUNGING ON THE sofa, reading the February issue of *Cosmopolitan* magazine. Joni was at the mirror trying to see if she could put dog ears in her hair.

Guys always pulled on Gina's when Gina had them, and Joni wanted to give it a whirl.

"Joni," Gina shouted into the hallway where the mirror was. "Check out my February horoscope. 'You're pleasure oriented, and now more than ever your desires can be satisfied.' I can tell that this is going to be a good month." Then

THERE CAME A KNOCK AT THE DOOR

"Door's open, I'm not jokin'. Come on in," Gina said, turning the page in her magazine.

"Hey, Gina, it's Wheeler. Is Joni home? And, I've brought a friend for you," Wheeler said, pointing to the tall, blond man behind him. "He's another driver and we've been team driving for the past few weeks. Just got back in from the East Coast. Gina, meet Charlie. Charlie, this is Gina, Joni's roommate."

"Well, hello big fella," Gina said, putting down her magazine and sitting up on the sofa. "I'm so glad you are meeting me for this first date. What *am* I going to wear? Oh, and would you like a mimosa?"

Charlie nodded, saying to Wheeler, "Isn't it a bit early for a mimosa?"

Wheeler laughed and threw his head back. "It's never too early to party with these girls!"

"Who is that I hear?" Joni yelled from the hallway. She had one dog ear and was working on the second one. "Wheeler?"

"Yup," Wheeler said, walking into the hallway. Joni screamed with joy and ran into his arms.

"What are you doing here?" she asked.

"We have a layover for a few days so I thought you and I and Charlie and Gina could do a little sightseeing here in Tempe."

"Joni, make us all a mimosa," Gina directed. "And what in the world is that hairdo you have going on? Looks like a one-eared dog."

Joni pulled the rubber band from her dog ear and raked her hair with her fingers. Gina was always right.

"I didn't see your car in the parking lot, Gina," Wheeler said.

"Well, you have good eyesight. It isn't there. Some creep stole it. We tried to report it to the police the day it happened and we may have been drunk when we went to the police station. The policeman on duty told us to wait ten days to do a police report. Ten days later, the policeman on duty told us it was probably in Mexico. Don't even start me on policemen right now. We're not talking about this again. Joni, get these boys a mimosa and another one for me."

Wheeler, like Joni, knew that if Gina said something, she meant it and you had better do what she says. He looked at Charlie and nodded slightly, and Charlie picked up on the hint.

Joni finished making the mimosas and handed them out, glasses for Gina, Wheeler, and Charlie, the plastic mug for herself. Wheeler had never gotten up the courage to ask why Joni had to drink out of plastic glasses and didn't think this was the time to bring it up.

"So how long are you here for?" Joni asked Wheeler, thinking of how she wanted to spend her time with him.

"The entire weekend. Whatever you had planned, we are all in for," Wheeler replied.

Gina turned her head to the side, eyeing Charlie and thinking he just might be what she needed this weekend. "Well, how about we go tubing today?"

"Tubing!" Charlie exclaimed. "What in the world is that?"

Gina and Joni laughed. Gina continued. "Well, you get a lot of beer and put it into a floating cooler, then you get the Tupperware container for snacks and whatever else and hook it to the Styrofoam top of another cooler. Then you hook it all together with rope and tie it to the inner tubes you sit on and float down the Salt River."

"What? Sounds nuts to me," Charlie said.

Wheeler turned to Charlie and shook his head. "I told you these girls were crazy!"

Gina picked up her Princess phone and called Bob and Jill. They needed someone else to go with them so they could park one car at the beginning of the tubing and another at the end. Bob and Jill said they would be over in an hour.

"Joni, my dear, while we're waiting for Bob and Jill you'd better make us more mimosas."

"Yes, Gina dear. Coming right up."

Fortunately, the boys both had cutoff jeans that they could wear for a swimming suit bottom. The girls always wore cutoffs when they were tubing because if the Salt River was a little low, your butt bounced around on the rocks. The girls wore bathing suit tops with the cutoffs.

Bob and Jill arrived shortly after the last mimosa.

"Looks like you girls have already started the party," Bob said.

Gina smiled. "Of course, Bob. Joni's friend Wheeler is here and he brought me his friend Charlie. We had to be hospitable, you know."

Joni finished putting the coolers in her truck. Wheeler and Charlie rode with Joni in her pickup. Gina went with Bob and Jill. The group stopped at the Circle K to buy canned beer and some ice for the coolers.

Charlie was still not convinced. When the girls went into the Circle K to buy the beer and ice, he looked at Wheeler and said, "Do you think we are crazy to do this?"

Wheeler laughed. "No, you are going to find out how much fun these girls are. Joni told me that the Salt River is not really a big river unless it is monsoon time, so even if you can't swim, you can stand up in it. We'll just have fun in the sun and drink beer."

"But what about the tubes?" Charlie asked. And this was when the girls returned to the truck to load up the beer from the Circle K.

"Not to worry," Gina said, having heard Charlie's question. "We'll stop by Peckerwood and pick up six tubes. They always keep some there because tubing is a big thing on weekends."

"Peckerwood?" Charlie said, then punched Wheeler on the shoulder. "What in the world did you get me into?"

Wheeler just laughed again. Once Charlie saw that Peckerwood was just where a bunch of guys lived, he relaxed a bit.

Jill and Bob had decided that Bob would park their car at the end of the tubing trip. Everyone would get in the back of Joni's pickup with the tubes and the coolers and she would park at the start of the tubing trip.

When Joni parked her truck and everyone got out, Charlie said, "Whoa, what a lot of people!"

"Yup," Gina said. "Everyone loves to tube the Salt."

"River," Jill added, knowing that not everyone knew that the Salt was the Salt River.

Taking Wheeler to the side, Charlie said, "Okay, I guess this is a fun thing to do. But where are the bathrooms?"

Gina overhead this and started laughing. "Silly boy, everyone just pees in the river!" she said, showing her dimples and smiling.

Bob helped Joni pull the coolers and the tubes from the back of her truck and locked it up. Joni tied a Styrofoam lid to the Tupperware container that held things that couldn't get wet, along with the car keys, and then attached that to her tube. Bob tied the Styrofoam beer cooler to his tube.

"You better not get too far ahead of us," Jill scolded.

"You better not," Gina added. "You have all the beer tied to you, Bob." Bob just laughed, daring them to stay with him.

Wheeler and Charlie looked on as the preparations continued.

"Sunscreen anyone?" Joni asked. She always burned badly when they tubed and had slathered herself with it.

"Not for me," Gina said. "My Indian blood keeps me from burning." Jill took some for her face. Wheeler and Charlie declined.

Finally, everyone was in the water in their tubes, joining the crowds of others in the river. Before they pushed off, everyone popped open a beer.

"Careful, people, don't throw your pop-tops in the river. Put them in your can or give them to Joni to put in the Tupperware," Jill said. "Too many people have gotten cut on the pop-tops. And remember how close your butt is to the river bottom if you need a reason to be careful."

"Your butt and other things women are interested in," Gina said, batting her eyelashes at Charlie.

Charlie blushed. He was certain he had never been around girls like Gina and Joni before.

The group floated along leisurely, enjoying a few beers and staying together. Wheeler and Joni had tied their tubes together. Charlie and Gina were holding hands. Bob knew better than to get too far ahead or face Jill's wrath.

"So how do you know when to get out?" Wheeler asked.

Gina answered. "We've tubed this river so many times that we know to get out right after the turn about an hour from here. The Salt doesn't go to the ocean, so you won't have to worry about that!"

Everyone laughed.

About an hour later, Gina turned to Charlie and said, "You are beginning to look a little red. Maybe you should have used some of Joni's sunscreen."

Charlie knew that his face was flushed but thought it was just the beer. "Oh well, we should be close to the end, right?"

"Well, maybe. Hey, Joni. Can you reach the sunscreen for Charlie?"

Joni reached into the Tupperware container and had Wheeler paddle them closer to Charlie's tube.

"Better use this now, dude, or you will pay tomorrow," Joni said, passing the sunscreen over to him. Charlie spread the sunscreen all over his face.

Not long after that, the group reached the end of their run. "Time to get to the shore on the left," Bob said, paddling that direction. Everyone followed. The river was shallow here, so close to the bank, everyone stood up and carried their tube to dry land. Joni got the Tupperware container and Bob got the cooler.

"Still some beer in here if anyone wants one while I take Joni up to get her truck," Bob said.

"And I made some corned beef sandwiches if anyone is hungry. They are in a plastic bag in the cooler," Jill announced.

Corned beef sandwiches? Gina thought. Well, better than nothing. There wasn't much to eat at the apartment, and she knew that the boys were going to be hungry.

Joni brought her pickup truck back to the place where the tubing had ended, and everyone helped to load things into the back. Joni even grabbed a corned beef sandwich, wishing Jill had brought mustard. Oh well, better than nothing, thinking the same thing as Gina.

After stopping to return the tubes at Peckerwood, Bob and Jill followed Joni to the Windbell to help unload the pickup and take everything upstairs.

"It was a great time," Wheeler said to the group.

"And my first time tubing," said Charlie, who by this time was red as a lobster. "Not something I will ever forget."

"Well, Charlie, my dear," Gina said, pulling his hand, "let me take you upstairs and tend to your sunburn. We have to get you in shape for skin on skin," she said, laughing and raising her eyebrows, which always brought out her dimples.

Charlie blushed but his sunburn was redder than his blush, so no one saw it.

Bob and Jill left to go home.

"Joni, you'd better take a shower quickly because I am going to tend to Charlie's sunburn. Take Wheeler with you if he wants one so you can save hot water," Gina instructed.

Wheeler looked at Joni and nodded. "We can make it fast," Joni replied.

Fast? Wheeler thought. Oh, she means the shower!

Joni and Wheeler were in and out of the shower in about five minutes. Gina had taken off Charlie's wet clothing and wrapped him in a towel.

"What now?" Joni asked.

"First, make us coffee with brandy. Then make me a cup of tea with two tea bags and leave the bags in the cup. Then bring me the oatmeal box," Gina said, pushing Charlie into the room that the bathtub and toilet were in. The sink and mirror were outside in the hallway to give everyone more privacy.

Wheeler told Joni that he would wait for her in the bedroom. While he hadn't gotten a sunburn like Charlie, he was tired from driving the night before and was ready to rest.

Joni made everyone a coffee and brandy, taking Wheeler's to him in the bedroom, Gina and Charlie's to the sink area and knocking on the door to the tub area. She left the oatmeal with their drinks.

She made the cup of tea with two tea bags as Gina instructed, took them to the sink area with the other drinks for Gina and Charlie, then cleaned up the kitchen. Afterward, she joined Wheeler in the bedroom with her own coffee and brandy after locking the apartment door. The girls were too busy with their truck drivers to deal with anyone else tonight.

"What are you doing?" Charlie shouted to Gina.

"Hush, little boy. Get in this warm tub and drink your coffee. I'm going to give you an oatmeal bath."

"But I barely know you, and you want me to take off this towel?"

Gina smiled as only Gina could smile. "Of course I want you to take off that towel. I know what's under it isn't sunburned but it would be awkward to get into the tub with a towel wrapped around you. I'm just going to make sure that the sunburned parts are better."

Charlie took off the towel. Gina liked what she saw. She poured the oatmeal into the cool water and swirled it around.

"Stay here and soak while I get the tea bags for your face."

"Tea bags?" Charlie barely said out loud as he relaxed in the tub.

"Yup. The tannic acid in the tea bags is going to help your eyes and your face with the sunburn."

Charlie had never heard of either of Gina's remedies, but Wheeler had convinced him not to argue with these girls.

As the tub drained, Charlie couldn't believe how much better he felt after the bath in oatmeal and soaking with tea bags on his face.

"I'm so much better," he said, thanking Gina.

"Good enough to go to bed?" Gina said.

"I thought you'd never ask!"

CHAPTER 22

Sunday, February 11. The release of American POWs (prisoners of war) had begun. This day is Staying Single Day, dancing through life without a partner. Legend has it that a group of single college students started this as Valentine's Day was just around the corner.

· ·

EVERYONE SLEPT IN THIS MORNING. Joni, as usual, was first up and put on the water for their morning coffee, without brandy. Wheeler woke next, walked to the sofa, and turned on the television for the news.

When the water started boiling on the stove, Joni let the whistle blow to wake Gina and Charlie. They stumbled out shortly thereafter.

"So, how's the sunburn?" Joni asked Charlie.

Charlie blushed. His sunburn was so less red that you could see him blush again. "So much better, thanks to Gina's magic cures."

"Gina," Joni said strongly. "Am I going to have to call the apartment manager and get the maintenance guy up here? I saw how much oatmeal you used in the bathtub and I know it is going to clog up the drain."

"Why don't we just see whose drain clogs up first. All the apartments go into the same drainpipe eventually. No need to tell them that it might be us who used an entire box of oatmeal in the bathtub."

"*Us?*" Joni said.

Gina just sighed. "Of course, Joni, dear. One for all, all for one, or however that goes."

Wheeler was laughing. Then he said to Charlie, "Hey, dude, glad to see that you are doing okay today. You were really red yesterday."

"Like you said, Wheeler, never doubt what these girls say." Charlie grinned and took Gina's hand in his, pulling her over to the sofa where Wheeler sat.

"So what's up for today, drivers?" Gina asked the boys.

"Not too much," Wheeler responded. "We have a long trip going out tomorrow and we have to be in good shape. How about a nice meal, a few drinks, and early to bed?"

"Early to bed? That's my favorite part," Gina said, looking into Charlie's eyes and showing her dimples.

"Hey, Gina, how about we watch the news, get dressed, and go over to the Duck and Decanter for our afternoon meal?" Joni asked.

"What a great idea," Gina responded. "You guys are really going to like this. It's a wine bar with great food and is surrounded by a huge garden nursery so you can sit outside at the tables and it feels like you are in the jungle."

"What about the sun?" Charlie asked, still feeling a bit of his sunburn and not wanting to get any more sun.

"Not to worry," Gina and Joni said at the same time. Gina continued. "The plants from the nursery blot out the sun. It's like sitting in a rainforest. And it shouldn't be too hot today."

The foursome spent the morning drinking coffee, then a mimosa, then finally dressing for the day.

"Uh, Gina," Joni said when they were together at the mirror. "How are we going to all fit into my truck to go to the Duck and Decanter?"

"Oops. I guess we take a taxi this time. That way we can drink more anyway. Are you up for that? And you *do* have a job tomorrow, right?"

"Yep. I'm still typing out at Fountain Hills."

Gina called for a taxi when everyone was ready, and they all went out by Broadway to wait for it. Gina asked for a van so that everyone would fit comfortably and was happy to see the Volkswagen bus taxi turn into the Windbell. The ride over the Camelback, just past Sixteenth Street, was fun as the boys got to see what Phoenix looked like.

"I never thought that the desert could be this beautiful," Wheeler said to Joni.

"I didn't either. The first time I drove here to see Gina I thought she was nuts, living here."

"And I never thought I'd find someone so beautiful in the desert," Wheeler continued, nudging Joni.

The taxi pulled into the parking lot at the Duck and Decanter. The girls were surprised when Wheeler paid the taxi fare. Usually the girls paid out the money for their fun.

"How long do you think we'll be here?" Wheeler asked the girls.

"How much do you want to drink?" Gina answered mischievously.

"So about two to three hours?" Wheeler guessed.

"Sure, that would be fine. We don't want Charlie to be out in the sun too long," Gina said, poking Charlie with her elbow. "And you guys have to get to bed early tonight."

Wheeler asked the taxi driver to be back at the Duck and Decanter in about three hours. The driver agreed, as Wheeler had given him a nice tip.

"Come on," Gina said, pulling Charlie's arm. "We go inside and order our food. A bottle of wine and whatever sandwich you want." Joni and Wheeler followed.

Once their orders were received and the bottle of wine chosen, the four went outside to sit at one of the tables on a gently rolling, grassy hill.

"It's just like you said, Gina, like sitting in a rainforest under the plants," Charlie said.

Wheeler agreed. "You don't even think about being in the desert sitting out here."

The girls just smiled. They knew the ambience that the Duck and Decanter had. They knew they had made the right choice of activities for a quiet Sunday afternoon.

The third bottle of wine was almost empty. Wheeler looked at his watch, saying, "Drink up, girls and boys. The taxi should be here in about five minutes."

Joni leaned over to Gina and said, "I have to go to the bathroom. You can finish my wine and I'll meet everyone out front."

Gina just shook her head, and of course agreed. She would always take care of Joni.

It was late afternoon when they got back to the Windbell. The boys took turns taking a shower so they would be ready for their long trip in the morning. After the showers, Joni made Gina's famous grasshopper concoction for everyone for their last drink of the day. Charlie grabbed Gina's arm and pulled her to the bedroom.

"Well," Wheeler said to Joni, "I guess that's our cue to go to bed. It's been a great day and I have a long ride coming up, so let's join your roomie and my co-driver in dreamland."

Joni smiled.

CHAPTER 23

Monday, February 12. The release of POWs in the Vietnam War began as three US Air Force C-141 medical transports landed at the Gia Lam Airport in Hanoi in North Vietnam to pick up American POWs. The Vietcong released another 27 American military and civilian prisoners who had been held captive in "jungle prisons" in Vietcong-controlled areas of South Vietnam. At the same time, a North Vietnamese Air Force C-9A transport was allowed to land in Saigon in South Vietnam to pick up North Vietnamese and Vietcong prisoners. The three aircraft brought 116 POWs to Clark Air Force Base in the Philippines on the first day of the operation. US Navy Captain Jeremiah Denton was appointed by his fellow prisoners to be the first of 41 prisoners to step off the first C-141 to land, followed by US Navy Lieutenant Commander Everett Alvarez Jr., who had been the first American POW captured in North Vietnam and who had been incarcerated since August 5, 1964.

. . . .

WHEELER AND CHARLIE HAD TO leave early to get back on the road. They had a load going to Vermont and then a load of paper driving to Texas to a check factory in San Antonio.

As the girls were getting ready for work, Gina said, "Well, Joni, looks like my horoscope came true! Would *Cosmo* ever lie to me?"

Joni laughed. "I'm glad you had such a good time with Charlie. At least this surprise was better than when Pilot brought you home the ex-football player."

"Don't remind me. I still remember the bruised ribs he caused. And remember we finally figured out he wasn't a football player because most football players don't have knife marks on their back."

"Pilot never was one to tell us the whole truth. Anyway, let's forget Pilot and remember what a few nice days we have had with the truck drivers."

"I could fall in love with him," Joni said wistfully, thinking of Wheeler.

"Joni, he's only another dick. And remember, you have Tom Dixon and Rudy and many more to be explored."

Joni shrugged. As usual, Gina was probably right.

CHAPTER 24

Saturday, February 17. US National Security Adviser Henry Kissinger meets Chinese leader Mao Zedong, where the latter jokingly offers to send ten million Chinese women to the United States.

. . . .

"JONI," GINA YELLED FROM THE kitchen, "get your ass out of bed. We need to go to Bashas' and fill up our larders again. We're out of liver and onions." And with that, Joni grimaced. "And we need more ice cream to make our frozen grasshoppers. Oh, and Joni, make a list. Remember that article from the January *Cosmopolitan* about the fresh avocado facial? We have to try that. We'll need a ripe avocado and a cup of sour cream for both of us."

"Gina, I don't remember what you are talking about."

Gina thought, Maybe you were drunk when I read it to you? But she replied anyway. "For each person, you take a half of a ripe avocado and add one-half cup of chilled sour cream. The article said 'Apply lavishly' and then after fifteen minutes, wash it off with 'tepid' water. What in the heck is 'tepid' water, since you were an English major?"

"Lukewarm. Who knows why they chose that word. And do we really have to wear a mashed vegetable on our faces?"

"Joni, Joni, we have to stay young. You know how you like those young things. So get moving, we need to go shopping."

Knowing that Gina meant what she said, Joni hurried to throw on a pair of wheat jeans and her brown top she really liked, thinking, Okay, okay, I know I wear this shirt all the time. She had worn them yesterday, but who was she going to see at the grocery store who might have seen her yesterday.

"Joni," Gina said, "good thing we have your truck because we have a lot of groceries to be buying."

Joni just shook her head. She knew there wouldn't be that much food because the girls didn't have that much money. Payday was next week.

At Bashas' the girls filled their cart with liver and onions—a staple at their Windbell apartment, the requisite vanilla ice cream for the girls' famous grasshopper drinks, some rice for moments when there wasn't anything else to eat, cottage cheese, eggs, bacon, and bread. After checking out, when the girls went to leave the grocery store, there was a table at the exit door with a woman dressed in all white.

"Girls," the woman said. "Are you interested in participating in a frozen French fry food test? All the frozen fries are free and your only cost is to partici-pate in a phone call for about fifteen minutes in four weeks."

Gina looked at Joni. Joni raised her eyebrows and looked back at Gina. Gina said, "*I love French fries!*"

The woman gave Gina four boxes of frozen French fries, each in a plain white unmarked box, saying, "Be sure to keep them frozen until you cook them. Then make notes on which ones you prefer and like the best and the reasons why."

Seemed simple. Gina thought, Free food, and maybe we can have a party around this one, accepting the four white boxes of frozen French fries and adding them to their grocery cart. Gina gave the woman their Windbell apartment phone number and names.

"Gina," Joni said. "We should have bought more ketchup. I can't eat French fries without ketchup."

Gina made the rat face at Joni. "Go get some tomorrow or after work on Monday. Your temp agency *is* going to find you something to do, right? The rent is coming due." Joni knew the rest and just shrugged.

When the girls got home, Joni rushed to put away the groceries. "Whoa, Joni," Gina said. "Where's the horse? You're not going anywhere until Monday, and you'd better be going somewhere Monday to work."

Joni hung her head. "Yup, I was hurrying to put away the groceries. I just remembered that I have the perfect song for the frozen French fry test."

Gina always enjoyed Joni's songs, so she said, "Okay, chickie, pick up the guitar and let me hear what you have."

Joni went to her bedroom and lovingly pulled out her Gibson LG-1 guitar, then went back into the living room and sat on the sofa, singing,

In eighteen hundred and forty-five
There wasn't hardly a man alive
Who had anything to eat but beans and salmon
Because of the potato famine
I'll tell you what really hap... pened

—*Joni's Songbook*
"The Potato Famine Song"

As Joni continued through the verses, Gina started laughing and couldn't stop. "Oh, Joni, that's so right on. You will have to sing it again when we try our frozen French fries. Maybe the frozen French fry company will buy your song for a commercial!"

"Well, wouldn't that just float my boat!"

CHAPTER 25

Tuesday, February 27. On the Pine Ridge Reservation in South Dakota, over two hundred members of
the Oglala Lakota tribe and others seized the town of
Wounded Knee, site of the infamous massacre of three
hundred Sioux by the US Seventh Cavalry in 1890.

. . . .

JONI WAS WATCHING THE EVENING news as Gina combed
her hair to get ready to go to The Hut. After all, it was
"*T* for Tuesday" and that always meant The Hut.

"Gina," Joni shouted into the hallway where the
mirror was. "The American Indian Movement just
occupied Wounded Knee in South Dakota. There
are two hundred Oglala Lakota Indians taking
over, saying that the United States isn't ful-
filling promises made in treaties. What
are we going to do about this?"

"Joni, I doubt 'we' are going to do
anything about this other than watching it on the news. But I am not surprised. I'm not a Lakota Indian, but as a

Cherokee, I can fully understand why the tribe is so upset about the treaties. Do you think Oklahoma was always full of white people?"

"Sorry, Gina, I know you have sympathy for all Indian tribes. Maybe we need to go up to the Pine Ridge Reservation and help them out."

"Joni, the only place we need to go right now is to The Hut and take in those sixty-five-cent pitchers of the coldest beer in Tempe."

Joni went over to their brick-and-board shelving unit that held their mayonnaise jar full of coins (as well as their stereo and the record albums) and counted out sixty-five pennies, which she wrapped in a red bandana. "Okay, Gina, I've got the money for the first pitcher."

"Great. I'm sure we'll find someone who will buy us the second one."

Joni drove because Gina still didn't have a car. The girls were surprised to find that there was a parking space available in front of The Hut, and Joni pulled into it. Walking into the bar, they noticed the regulars there but none of the fraternity boys who usually gathered there on Tuesdays.

"Hey, Florina," Gina said to the bartender, "where are the frat boys?"

Florina just laughed. She knew that Gina and Joni weren't fond of the frat boys anyway and said, "Having some big frat boy thing over on campus. I'll miss their tips but I won't miss their disgusting drunken behavior. You remember last year when one of them challenged a pledge to drink a whole glass of hot sauce?

He drank it but he sure made a mess throwing it right back up."

The girls laughed, ordered their pitcher of beer, and settled down to see what would happen next. Boyer and Pete Groat were playing pool. Caffy was sitting at one of the booths watching Boyer's ass. The television was showing some sports show, as Florina said that Vince was going to stop by. Vince only allowed the bartenders to show sports on the television, so the bartenders were sure to have sports on when they knew he would come in.

"Gina," Joni said, "I think this is boring. I'd rather go home and read a good book."

"We could always cruise down Mill Avenue."

"Yup, but I'm not sure I'm up to anything tonight."

Just then the front door opened, and in walked Tom Dixon and Benson.

"Hello, girls, just who we were looking for!" Benson said.

Gina and Joni perked up. Two of their favorite men had just walked into The Hut.

"What can I get you for?" Gina asked, putting her fingers in her dimples, smiling and tilting her head.

Benson just smiled. "You can get me for nothing," he answered, tilting his head the same as Gina.

Tom Dixon just walked up to Joni and put his arm around her shoulders. "Join you for a beer?" he said. Joni just nodded and Tom Dixon asked Florina for another pitcher and two more glasses.

"So what's shakin', bacon?" Gina asked the boys.

"Not much," Tom Dixon answered. "The Fireside Lounge was pretty empty tonight so my happy hour performance was over early. We thought we'd come over to Tempe and see if anything was happening here."

"Not much," Gina answered, "but we could certainly spice things up if you are interested."

Both boys laughed. "Sure," Benson said. "Let's drink up this beer and go up the street for some dancing."

Joni was ready for some time with Tom Dixon, so her desire to go home and read a book faded quickly. Benson sat next to Gina and the two of them talked between themselves. Tom Dixon sat next to Joni, saying, "I really miss you when you aren't at my happy hour shows."

Joni smiled. "I'll try to make it to more of them. I don't really know where my temp agency is going to send me unless I am on a long-term assignment. At least you know where to find us!"

Gina turned to Joni and said, "Hey, chickie, Benson is going to a craft fair in New Mexico and I may get to go with him. You know how I love my craft shows."

"Cool beans, Gina," she replied. "But let's drink up and get these boys to the music where we can do some dancing."

All four of them emptied their glasses, and the group left to walk up Mill Avenue to The Cave. In addition to music, The Cave had twenty-five-cent tequila shots on Tuesdays. As they got to the door they heard "Do You Want to Dance" by Bette Midler. Tom Dixon turned to Joni and nodded his head, taking her hand and pulling her into the club and onto the dance floor. Benson and Gina went to the bar to order drinks, of course tequila shots all the way around.

Benson looked at Gina and said, "Do you really think you could get away to go to the New Mexico Arts and Crafts Fair in Albuquerque? It's held at the state fairgrounds and we could find a cheap motel close to there. We'd have a great road trip and a lot of fun."

"Heck yes, I want to go!" Gina said, gushing. "I assume you would be taking your van with all your supplies, right?" The girls still had not told anyone except Wheeler and his friend Charlie about Pucci being stolen.

"You bet, Gina. We could even sleep in the van but I think you would enjoy a motel bed better." Gina was thinking that she would enjoy any bed with him. "Okay then, I'll get the dates and we can make plans later."

With that, Gina downed her shot of tequila and ordered one more round for the group. Gina and Benson had secured four barstools and were saving two of them for Joni and Tom Dixon.

The music changed to "Could It Be I'm Falling in Love" by The Spinners. Joni softly sang along with the words, thinking maybe she could fall in love with this guy, even though she hadn't known him very long.

"Do you want to keep dancing, Joni?" Tom Dixon asked.

"I think we should go suck down our tequila shots and see what happens. Do you think you can stop by the Windbell before you go back into Phoenix?"

"Nothing would suit me better," he answered as he pulled Joni over to the bar. "Drink up, Joni."

"You two are dancing fools," Gina said. "Joni, I think I'm going to catch a ride with Benson and head on home to the Windbell. See you later, alligator."

"In a while, crocodile," Joni said in response. It was an exchange the girls said frequently.

Gina and Benson left the bar and walked back to The Hut where Benson's van was parked.

After Gina and Benson left The Cave, Joni and Tom Dixon drank their tequila shots, looking each other in the eye. Joni couldn't wait to get Tom Dixon home but didn't want to appear too eager. Trying to be casual, she said, "Why don't we go back to my place and I'll slip into something more comfortable." Joni was good at clichés.

"Joni, I'd rather you didn't slip into anything at all," he said, taking her hand and pulling her back to The Hut on the sidewalk by Mill Avenue. "Oh, Benson's truck is still here so they must be inside. Gina had mentioned something about one more beer. But I'm through partying, so let's just go to your place. You know I can't stay all night but I'll stay as long as I can."

Joni was all for that. She'd take what she could get of him.

Back at the Windbell, Joni opened the door and took Tom Dixon back to her bedroom. Later, they heard the front door open with Gina's laugh as she and Benson stumbled into the living room.

It was another wonderful night at the Windbell apartment.

Part Three

MARCH 1973

You come to me in the morning
As the sunlight marks the day
And you fill me with your magic
In a very special way
I want you every evening
I want you all night long
But I know someone else owns you
And you have to go home
So I'll just keep you in my heart
And forever in my song
Keep you in my heart
And forever in my song

—Joni's Songbook

CHAPTER 26

Thursday, March 1. Pink Floyd's eighth studio album, *The Dark Side of the Moon*, was released. Robyn Smith rode North Sea in a New York City horse race to become the first woman jockey to win a stakes race.

. . . .

WHEELER HAD SHOWN UP AT the apartment at 7:00 a.m. He knocked on the door and Joni answered as she was getting ready for work.

"Joni, I just got off the road. Been driving all night. Can I crash here today? I'd stay at Rudy's house but he has Martha over and the place is full of guys and gals seeing who can make the most noise."

"Joni," Gina shouted from the hallway. "I hope you are ready because you need to drop me off at work this morning."

"Gina, not to worry. Wheeler's here and he wants to crash here all day if that's okay with you."

"Sure, Joni. Hey, Wheeler. Did you bring me another trucker again?" Gina laughed to herself.

"Sorry, Gina, it's just me. Why don't I order a pizza this afternoon when I wake up and treat you girls to dinner? Just bring home some beer to go with it." Wheeler was so tired he walked straight into Joni's bedroom, stripped to his undies, and flopped on the bed.

"Well," Gina said, "at least we have someone to guard our castle today, although I'm not sure how much good a passed-out truck driver will be."

"Come on, Gina, let's get you to work. I'll pick you up right at five, we'll grab the beer, and head on home for pizza."

Gina walked to the doorway of Joni's bedroom and yelled, "Hey, Wheeler, you'd better make it two pizzas. You never know who is going to show up here when we get home that early."

Wheeler grunted as he was sleeping, and Gina took that as a yes. The girls walked out the door and down the stairs to Joni's truck in the parking lot.

After dropping Gina off at work, Joni drove over to her temp job for the day on Seventh Avenue, not too far from Gina's office, where she was told she would be working in an insurance office, much like the one where Gina worked. Or at least that was what she thought it would be like. Instead, she ended up in a small insurance office where the owner thought Joni was his full-time maid. During the course of the day, she picked up dry cleaning, ironed a shirt that had become too wrinkled for his liking for a meeting with the landlord he had that afternoon, picked up lunch from a deli a few blocks away, cleaned his private bathroom, straightened up his office, and shopped for a birthday gift for his wife. She couldn't wait until it was five o'clock.

As Joni got ready to leave the office, the owner shouted, "Hey, you, will you be back here tomorrow?"

Joni thought with any luck, no, but instead replied, "I'll check with my agency. I don't know if they have me scheduled anywhere else. They will let you know," she said, crossing her fingers and almost running out the door.

"You wouldn't believe this day," Joni said to Gina as soon as she was in the pickup truck, and proceeded to tell Gina the housekeeping chores of the day. At least she was getting paid.

The girls stopped at the Circle K to pick up a few six-packs of beer, then hurried home to see what was going on there. When they opened the door to the apartment, there sat Wheeler and Benson at the gateleg table playing cards. Benson smiled his largest smile, turned to Gina, and said, "I hope you don't mind me showing up without notice, Gina."

Gina smiled right back, shaking her head with her dimples going side to side, then rushed over to Benson for a big hug.

"Where's the pizza, Wheeler?" she said firmly, as Benson hugged her. "Joni has the beer and she'll keep it cold."

"I thought I'd wait to order until you girls got home. Shouldn't take long to get here," Wheeler answered, not wanting to incur the wrath of Gina.

"*Fine. Fine, fine, fine*," Gina said, using one of her favorite phrases when she wasn't really happy about things. "Joni, get us all a beer, dear," she shouted into the kitchen where Joni was putting up the beer.

"Anything you say, *dear* Gina," Joni quipped, knowing Gina was over it by then.

Gina walked into her bedroom, changed from her work clothing to jeans and a frilly blouse, then went back to the living room and plopped onto the sofa, picking up the March *Cosmopolitan*. Wheeler called to order the pizza and then continued his card game with Benson. Joni just made sure everyone had a cold drink.

"Hey, Wheeler," Gina said, looking up from her magazine. "Listen to this from an article about whether or not men should do women's work. It says that they asked a twenty-four-year-old truck driver about his opinion on this subject. His response was 'If I could find some good-looking broad who would support me, I'd stay at home and watch TV and eat all day long.'"

Wheeler and Benson started laughing at this.

"Don't start me on this, Wheeler, or you either, Benson. Sexist pigs. Do you think women just sit at home and watch TV and eat bonbons all day long?" Gina grumbled. "This is the seventies. Women work. Women have brains. Women do what they want to do."

"Ah, Gina," Benson interrupted, "that's what I like about you. You take no shit from anyone and you are at the forefront of the sexual revolution. Which we can probably verify later after we eat the pizza!"

Gina relaxed. "Okay, Benson, I'll take you up on that verification! But pizza first. I gotta have my strength."

The pizza soon arrived, and everyone ate their fill. Benson and Gina retired to her bedroom, each with a shot of brandy. Joni stayed in the kitchen to clean up.

"So, Wheeler, what's up now?" Joni asked. "You've been asleep all day so you should be rested up."

"I have another load going out in a few hours, and I'm not sure when I'll be back this way, but of course you'll be the first to know. I thought I'd like to spend those few hours with you. Is that okay with you?"

"Hmmm," Joni hummed, "let me think that over." She had a serious face but was laughing inside. Wheeler wasn't quite sure what was going on.

"It's a joke, driver! Get your butt into my bedroom and get it out of those pants!"

Wheeler stood up, picked up Joni, and once again carried her to her bedroom. They enjoyed his few hours at the Windbell the same as ever.

CHAPTER 27

Friday, March 2. US federal forces surrounded Wounded Knee, South Dakota, which was occupied by members of the militant American Indian Movement who were holding at least ten hostages. The first four female US Navy pilots begin training.

· ·

JONI WOKE FIRST IN THE morning and called her temp agency. "Do I have to work at that insurance agency again? All I did was things a maid or a wife do."

The temp agency said that no, she didn't have to go there unless she wanted to but they didn't have any other jobs open for that day. Joni thought that a crummy job was better than no job so said she would return to the insurance office.

"Wake up, Gina," she shouted toward Gina's bedroom. "I have to go back to the hellhole of an insurance office and I'll need to drop you off first."

"Not to worry, Joni," Gina replied. "Benson will take me to work. You just be there at five to pick me up and we can go to The Hut after work. After all, it's Friday and we need to start the weekend off right."

"Ten-four," Joni said, having picked up the trucker language from Wheeler. Ten-four meant "okay."

After another day of doing personal errands for the owner of the insurance agency, Joni picked up Gina at work and the girls headed to The Hut. As usual on a Friday night, the place was crammed full of people, mostly men, including the frat boys. Nonetheless, Gina and Joni were able to find two stools at the bar. Florina had seen them come into The Hut and already had their pitcher poured. She set it down with two glasses and three coasters.

After a chilling swig of The Hut's coldest beer in town, Gina set her glass down on the bar with a chunk and said, "Oh no, Joni. It's been almost a month since we got those frozen French fries and this is the night the sponsor is supposed to call us to set up the time for the call when we make our report. We gotta be home for that. Which means we also have to cook them tomorrow. You know we can't eat all those fries so we'll just have to make a party of it."

"Works for me," Joni said.

"Hey, you, Boston Jack," Gina said when Boston Jack finished his turn at the pool table. "Wanna come over to our apartment tomorrow and participate in the frozen French fry test?"

Boston Jack shrugged and said, "Sure, whatever that is. I'll be over about noon then with some beer," then went back to his pool game.

"Hey, Joe Ravioli, come here," Gina continued. "Wanna come over to our apartment tomorrow and participate in the frozen French fry test?"

Joe said, "Sure," thinking, Whatever that is, it will be a hoot with these girls. "I'll bring some wine."

"Be there early afternoon," Joni said. "We have to get in the mood before the French fry people call." Joe Ravioli was perplexed. He scrunched his brow but said nothing because it was Gina and Joni.

"Okay," he said. "I'll be there on time." He thought, Whatever "on time" meant.

"Drink up, Joni," Gina said, nudging Joni in the side. "We gotta go home and get ready for that phone call we expect tonight. We can eat leftover pizza from yesterday and drink the rest of the beer."

Joni chugged down what was left in her glass, thinking, Good thing I like leftover pizza and glad the boys didn't drink all the beer. After all, *Peter Pan* with Mary Martin was showing on NBC tonight and it was one of Joni's all-time favorite movies. What could be better—leftover pizza, beer, and Peter Pan.

CHAPTER 28

Saturday, March 3. A US flag flies upside down outside a church occupied by members of the American Indian Movement on the site of the 1890 massacre at Wounded Knee. Roberta Flack wins a Grammy for her version of "The First Time Ever I Saw Your Face" by Ewan MacColl.

. . . .

"JONI," GINA SAID. "WE NEED to cook and eat those fries. And all four boxes. I don't know that you and I can eat all that many fries. We already invited The Hut people so let's just make a party out of it and invite the boys downstairs."

Gina went downstairs to Rudy's apartment and knocked on the door. "Woo-hoo, boys. Come out, come out, wherever you are," she said, putting her fingers into the dimples on both of her cheeks.

The door cracked open and Rudy said, "What in the world, Gina? We're still recovering from Friday night."

"We are having a party to check out the frozen French fry challenge that Joni and I are doing. The sponsor is calling us in a bit and we have to have everyone's input. A lady at Bashas' gave us four boxes of frozen French fries last time we were shopping there and asked us to evaluate them. The French fries are already in the oven and need to be eaten and judged. The lady will call us today for our answers. Plus, Joni is making us grasshoppers and I have shots of tequila for everyone, so let's get the party started! Oh, and Joe Ravioli is bringing wine and others are bringing beer."

Joe Rockefeller had heard Gina talking in the breezeway and opened the door to his apartment. "Can I come along, too?" Gina thought, What the hey, and just nodded. Joe Rockefeller could be a pain when he got too drunk, but for the most part he was just one of the Windbell people.

Soon the girls' apartment was filled with men. The Hut invitees arrived first, then Rudy and the boys from downstairs came up to join the party. Joni had made a blender full of their special ice cream grasshoppers and set out the party cups on the gateleg table for everyone to sample.

Then she finished baking the four boxes of frozen French fries, each on a different pan. Gina had a fresh bottle of tequila and was serving everyone shots in her Depression glass etched shot glasses. Except Joni—Joni was a klutz and had to have her tequila shots in a plastic shot glass.

The four pans of French fries were put out on the counter in the kitchen and Gina gave everyone a paper plate to sample the fries. Joni had indeed scored some ketchup, which everyone used. And plenty of salt. The boys were all laughing and eating when

THERE CAME A RING ON THE PHONE

"This is it," Gina said. "Joni, answer the phone."

"Hello, this is Joni."

"Hello, this is Myrtle calling about the frozen French fry potatoes. How are you today?"

Joni almost choked on her drink. "Well, we're having a party, tasting your four kinds of frozen French fries."

"Great," Myrtle said, apparently not picking up on what was going on.

"So," she continued, "what do you think about the four potato choices that you were given?"

Laughter erupted in the apartment. Gina tried to make the boys stop by flapping her arms, and that only served to make them laugh harder.

Joni took Gina's arm and said, "Girl, give it up. We have to tell this lady what we think of her potatoes. Po-*tah*-toes." That only started more laughter.

"Okay, okay," Myrtle continued. "Input please?"

Joni took it upon herself to answer. "Well, Myrts, the crinkle fries are our favorite because they hold the salt the best. The regular straight fries hold no salt and they don't even hold ketchup. The ridges are the best on the crinkly ones. The waffle fries are cute but really, oval-shaped French fries? And the shoestrings—yuk, too crispy, more like potato strings in a can."

The boys all hooted and slugged back another shot of tequila after Gina filled their shot glasses as Joni was talking to Myrtle.

Myrtle coughed and said, "Well, thank you for your input and, uh, I don't think we will be needing anything more from you, uh, and your friends."

By this time everyone was pretty much drunk on the tequila and laughing hysterically about the conversation with the French fry lady.

"Oval-shaped French fries?" Boston Jack said, shaking his head. "Where did they come up with that?"

"Creative geniuses. They're everywhere, they're everywhere," Joni replied, laughing and throwing back the rest of her tequila shot.

"Well, Miss Gina, I am a creative genius in my own way," Jack said.

"What are you talking about?" Gina replied. "I've never seen anything creative about you, much less a genius. I'm not from the 'Show Me' state, but show me, dude."

Jack smirked and turned his head to the side. "Sit on the chair at the gateleg table and take off your shoes."

This had gotten everyone's attention. The laughter stopped and they were all looking at Jack and then at Gina, wondering what was going to happen.

Gina huffed, then walked over to the gateleg table, sat at one of the chairs, and pulled off her shoes. "What now brown cow?"

Boston Jack looked perplexed.

"Gina was a drama major in college," Joni told everyone. "She used to have to lie down on the floor on her back and slowly say 'how now brown cow' over and over, and I guess she never got over that."

That started everyone laughing again. Then Boston Jack walked over to Gina, sat on the floor at her feet, and said, "Ever had your toes sucked?"

Chatter erupted in the drunken room. Toe sucking? Is he kidding? What was going on?

Gina shook her head. Boston Jack took Gina's left foot in his hands, and then took her second toe into his mouth. The room was quiet until Gina started humming, "Mmmmmmmmmm."

"Told you so," Boston Jack said triumphantly. "It's one of the greatest foreplay moves ever!" Now everyone was once again laughing.

Later the tequila bottle was empty, the frozen French fries eaten, and everyone was ready to go home. Fortunately, Joe Ravioli had drunk only one tequila, so he could drive Boston Jack and the other people from The Hut back to the bar. The rest of the boys stumbled downstairs to their own apartments.

"Joni," Gina said when everyone had gone. "I'm not sure I want to eat frozen French fries again." She wobbled into her room, falling onto her bed fully clothed, and passed out.

Joni cleaned up the party mess before going to bed herself, thinking, Well, it was one hell of a party.

CHAPTER 29

Sunday, March 4. Air Force Colonel Dewey Wayne Waddell was released from the Hanoi Hilton. His plane was shot down on July 5, 1967.

· · · · · · · · · · · · · · · · · · · ·

"JONI," GINA YELLED WHEN SHE woke up, "you'd better get me some coffee quickly if you want me to survive. And bring the aspirin."

Joni was already in the kitchen and had the water heating up. She had taken her aspirin an hour earlier.

With coffee in hand, Joni walked into Gina's bedroom. "Here you are, sunshine. And not to worry, I stayed up late last night and cleaned the kitchen."

Gina just scrunched up her face. She didn't plan to do much more that day but lie in bed, read magazines, and rest. She knew that *M*A*S*H* was on that evening and a new *Colombo* movie, so she was hoping to be awake for that.

"So, whaddya want to do today?" Joni asked.

"Nothing, Joni. I want to stay in bed, read magazines, and nap. Some of my favorite TV shows are on this evening. Plus, tomorrow is back to work for me. Do you have anything lined up for tomorrow?"

Joni shook her head. "I'll call first thing in the morning. Hopefully, the agency will find something for me to do. If you want to stay in all day, that's fine with me. I'll even do the laundry for both of us."

Gina smiled. Joni was always trying to please her.

CHAPTER 30

Monday, March 5. All the news shows were covering yesterday's press conferences where the surprise announcement that Yankees pitchers Peterson and Kekich had swapped wives was made.

. . . .

JONI WOKE UP GINA, THEN put on the water to boil for coffee and got dressed to take Gina to work. When she returned to the apartment, she called her temp agency to find out if they had any work for her. The only thing available was at the Holiday Inn, once again making beds and being a maid.

"I'll take it. Let them know I'm on my way." At least she didn't have to change clothing because the hotel provided the maid's uniform. And also, the job ended at 4:00 p.m. so she could easily get to Gina's job in time to pick her up.

Joni's day was about as exciting as watching a washing machine go around, but she handled it better than last time. At 4:00 p.m., she changed into her regular clothing and headed out to pick up Gina at her work.

Gina was already out on the sidewalk as Joni pulled up, looking a bit tired. She got into Joni's truck and closed the door.

"So what do you want to do now?" Joni asked. "Beefigger, The Hut, home?"

Gina looked at Joni. "I'm tired, Joni. Even spending the day yesterday in bed didn't get me back to normal. Besides, we've been drinking and eating too much. I think we should take this week off, get on a diet, and stay home."

Joni nodded her agreement. She, too, had been feeling her jeans being a little too tight.

"Well, at least I have work, although I'm scheduled for the Holiday Inn for the whole week. That can be my exercise because I am on my feet all day long."

Gina laughed. "Let's stop at Bashas' on the way home. We need more liver and onions, a carton of eggs, some spinach, and maybe lettuce and carrots. We'll jump-start this dieting week."

The girls spent the next few days going to work, coming home, and walking up and down the stairs to their second-floor apartment several times a day. Exercise, Gina had said, so Joni told herself that she really enjoyed walking up and down the stairs each time.

That week they ate their liver and onions, a chef's salad with boiled eggs, and a tuna fish salad with boiled spinach on the side. Joni was sure that her jeans were fitting better than ever. She was also missing the nightlife. She was sure that Gina was, too, but didn't dare ask.

On Wednesday they watched *The Sonny and Cher Comedy Hour*. Joni was sure that she looked like Cher. They both had prominent noses.

CHAPTER 31

Thursday, March 8. The US government and the Indians who took over Wounded Knee were both hoping for a ceasefire. Some residents of the city evacuated as they expected violence. Methodist bishop James Armstrong was finally able to get the two sides to agree to a cease-fire so that the two sides could continue negotiating.

• • • • • • • • • • • • • • • • • • • •

AS USUAL, JONI DROPPED GINA off at work, did her hours at the Holiday Inn back in Tempe, and then picked Gina up. Today Gina was smiling as Joni pulled up in front of her office building.

"I think we've dieted enough," Gina said, jumping into Joni's truck. I think we need a night off. Let's head for The Hut."

Joni smiled. She couldn't agree more.

The Hut was packed as Joni drove in and parked in the back, asking Gina if she was okay going to The Hut in their work clothing.

Gina scrunched up her nose. "Of course. You know they will all be wondering where we were for the last four days. They won't be looking at our clothing. They'll be looking for answers," she said, smiling and raising her eyebrows. "So what do you think we should tell them?"

"Well, we certainly don't want to say we were at a fat farm. How about that we were at a health spa?"

"Joni, no one in their right mind is going to believe that you and I had enough money to go to a health spa. How about telling them that we were on a Zen retreat?"

Joni shook her head side to side. "I doubt they are going to believe that, either. If anyone asks, why not just say that we were home for a few days? Sometimes the truth works, even if no one believes it."

Gina nodded her head. "Yes, let's tell the truth. No one has ever believed it in the past, so why should they start now? We've always told the truth about our escapades and everyone thought we were making it up."

"Like the time you and Carla were hitchhiking back from San Francisco to Austin at private airports? Or the time you and Carla were riding with the trucker who let you out at Gila Bend because you wouldn't sleep with him? And then him telling you that the desert was full of rattlesnakes."

By this time Gina was laughing so hard she could barely talk. "Yep, and Carla and I just danced like crazy, stomping our feet and making loud noises so the rattlesnakes would be scared. At least it was only a few hours before someone picked us up again. What adventures we had going back and forth from Austin to San Francisco."

Joni had not been part of those adventures, but she enjoyed the stories. She believed them even if no one else did.

"So let's go into The Hut and boogie," Gina said, interrupting Joni's reverie.

Shouts of "They're here" were heard as the girls walked into The Hut through the back door. Joe Ravioli rushed over to the girls and asked where they had been. Craig from Colorado just wanted to know if they were okay. Boyer was sitting with Caffy and did little more than pay attention to what everyone else was saying. Leroy B. jumped up and yelled to Florina, "Buy these girls a pitcher of beer on me."

Joni leaned in to Gina and whispered, "Gee, I guess we were missed more than we thought. Maybe we should do this again some time."

Gina just smiled and perched on a barstool, waiting for her cold beer. Joni joined her as soon as people stopped hugging her.

Florina put down the pitcher of beer, two glasses, and three coasters. "We've missed you. Quite a bit going on here."

Gina leaned forward. "How's tricks?" she asked. Florina looked confused. Gina continued. "So what's the scoop?" Florina still looked confused.

"Gina, my main language is Spanish. I'm not all into English phrases. I think, though, that you want me to tell you what's been going on."

"Oops, sorry, Florina. Yes, what's been going on?"

"Well, first Leroy B. got married. To a fifteen-year-old Mexican cutie who is apparently pregnant with his child."

Gina and Joni raised their eyebrows. Gina said, "We didn't even know he had a young girlfriend."

"Well, she's so young he can't bring her into the bars so no one has seen her. But apparently, they are in love so things may just work out okay."

"And what else?" Gina asked.

"Other than the usual, the big thing is that John-John was busted for drugs under the Salt River Bridge and they have taken him to jail in Safford."

"Safford? Where is that?"

"It's about three hours east of Phoenix. They took him there because it is a minimum security prison and he only had enough pot on him for the lightest sentence."

Joni shook her head. She cared about John-John. "Was he able to take his comic books with him?" she asked.

"Who knows," Florina said. "But he is allowed to have visitors.

"Okay," Gina said emphatically, "down the line, we're going to visit him and take him some comic books."

The girls drank up their pitcher and ordered another one. Gina was ready to go home, and Joni agreed. "More liver for dinner?" she asked.

"Nope, I think we deserve a quick stop at the Dash Inn for a hamburger or cheese crisp. We don't want to get too healthy this week!"

"Uh, Gina," Joni said. "I think we need to stay on our diet for a few more days. How about we stay home until next week? I need to save money for the rent next month and I'd like to lose another few pounds."

"Okay, Joni, I agree. So eat up tonight. Tomorrow I'm making more liver and onions. Breakfast is going to be little more than a white cross. You can take your instant soup for your lunch. Besides, nothing is going on this weekend that I know of. We'll just keep the door locked."

A quick stop at the Dash Inn—burger for Gina, cheese crisp for Joni, two more mugs of beer—and the girls were home for the evening. And the weekend after Friday at work.

CHAPTER 32

Monday, March 12. US President Richard Nixon announced that he was expanding the protection of executive privilege, the means in which the US president and staff were immune from having to testify or answer questions about White House events while in office, and said that it applied to former staff members as well. The last airing of *Rowan & Martin's Laugh-In* was shown on NBC TV.

. . . .

"DO YOU HAVE A JOB today?" Gina asked Joni.

"Not sure, but I'll stop at my temp agency after I drop you off at work. If nothing else I'll tell them I'll go back to the Holiday Inn even if I have to be a maid again. At least doing that I'm done by four and I can come pick you up after your work."

"Joni, make me some coffee and toast for breakfast," Gina said, walking to the sofa and picking up the March *Cosmopolitan.*

Joni put the water on to boil and as usual, pulled out two mugs and added a spoonful of Kava instant coffee, then stuffed two pieces of toast into the toaster.

"Listen to this, Joni. My March horoscope says that there is an Aries man out there who is dying to get married. And it says that Aries is a good match for my sign."

Joni poured the boiling water into the coffee mugs, buttered the toast, added a slice of cheese to each piece, and set breakfast on the table. "I don't know much about Aries men, but *Cosmo* has been right on most of the time."

Joni drove Gina to work and then stopped at her temp agency, which was on the way back to the apartment. The agency did not have a job for Joni that day but told her that tomorrow she could start typing at Arizona State University in the Speech and Theatre Department as one of their usual secretaries was going on vacation. The agency also told Joni that it might be a long-term job, maybe as much as a month. Joni jumped on it. She spent the day cleaning the apartment, even taking Gina's dirty clothing to the washing machine in their building. She knew Gina was always happy when not having to do her own laundry.

At four thirty, Joni left the apartment to pick up Gina and arrived just as Gina was walking out of her building. "Hey, Gina, do you want to stop at the Beef Rigger for a drink and eat the free food and listen to Tom Dixon for a bit?"

"I'm all for that. Maybe Benson will be there, too, although he usually only does sound when Tom Dixon is at the Fireside Lounge, but he could just be hanging out there. Fingers crossed."

Joni carefully pulled into the parking lot at the Beef Rigger and backed into a parking space.

"Joni, last time you backed into a parking space was in Pilot's car and you hit the light pole and dented the bumper."

"Well, yeah, but I've been practicing. Besides, I have a heavy-duty bumper on my truck so it won't matter."

Gina laughed.

Joni finished backing up and pulled the parking brake on. "See, I didn't hit anything."

Tom Dixon was on stage as the girls walked in. The Beef Rigger had its own soundman, but Benson was there anyway. Both boys smiled as they saw the girls walking in. Gina's dimples were showing as she smiled back at Benson. They joined him at his table.

After ordering a double John Collins for Joni and herself, Gina asked Benson, "So what are you doing here on a Monday evening?"

"I just wanted to see Tom Dixon sing once before I left town for a bit. Remember I mentioned that craft fair to you a few weeks ago? Looks like it will be very good for my business so I'm totally pumped about going. People in New Mexico like silver and turquoise almost as much as people in Arizona."

"Wow," Gina said, tilting her head, "that sounds like great fun."

"Would you still like to go with me? I leave tomorrow and I'll be back next Sunday."

"Heck yes, I want to go!" Gina said, tilting her head the other direction and smiling as only Gina can smile.

"Are you sure you can get off work?" Benson asked.

"For you, Benson, I'll definitely take off work! I have a lot of vacation days." Then to Joni, she said, "Are you going to be okay by yourself all week?"

"Yup. Tomorrow I start a job typing at the university that may be for a few weeks or maybe even a month or more. Without you here I may not spend as much time at The Hut so I can be sharp at this job."

"Cool beans," Gina exclaimed. "Benson, we're going to The Hut when we leave here for a few cold beers, then I'm going home to pack. I'll give notice to my boss in the morning."

Smiling, Benson said, "This will be a wonderful adventure. You are going to love the craft fair and you have never seen as much turquoise and silver jewelry in one place." Benson knew that Gina loved turquoise and silver jewelry.

"Ah, Benson, can I ask you a personal question?" Joni said.

"Sure, things are pretty personal with you girls!" Benson said, thinking about the nights he had spent with Gina. Joni scrunched up her eyes like she often did when she was contemplating what to do.

"So, what's your sign?" Joni finally said.

Benson laughed. "I haven't been asked that in a long time! I'm an Aries."

Gina and Joni looked at each other, eyes wide open. Maybe *Cosmo was* always right.

Tom Dixon finished his set and stopped at a few tables to greet members of the audience. Then he joined the girls and Benson at their table.

"Hello, girls. What's going on with you two wonderful women?"

Gina was bubbling and quickly said, "I'm going with Benson to a craft fair in New Mexico tomorrow. I can't wait."

Turning to Joni, Tom Dixon said, "And what are you going to be doing while Gina is gone with Benson? I only see you two girls together."

"Not to worry. I start a job at the university tomorrow that could last a week or a lot more, and the Speech and Theatre Department is not too far from The Hut, so I'll be entertained."

"I think I can help with that entertaining part. How about I stop by The Hut after I finish my set at the Fireside Lounge tomorrow?"

Joni smiled. "Nothing I'd like better!" Tom Dixon returned to the stage with a wave to the girls, who were just getting ready to leave.

"See you in the morning, Benson," Gina said.

"You bet, Red Rider!"

Once the girls were in Joni's truck, Gina said, "Let's blow off The Hut. I have a lot of packing to do and I have to do laundry."

"You're in luck, Gina. I did all your laundry while you were at work today."

"Great news! Then we do have time for one cold beer at The Hut. Or maybe one cold pitcher. Then we'll go home and you can help me pack."

CHAPTER 33

Tuesday, March 13. After spending more than five years in a North Vietnamese camp, Lieutenant Colonel Robert L. Stirm is reunited with his family at Travis Air Force Base in California.

. . . .

JONI LEFT THE APARTMENT EARLY to get to her new temp job at the university, hugging Gina and trying not to cry because Gina would be gone for almost a week.

"Stiff it up, Joni. You'll be fine. You have the boys downstairs, The Hut, and now it sounds like Tom Dixon might be around more often. Be happy."

"As Wheeler once said, 'Catch you on the flip-flop.'" And with that, Joni left for work.

Benson stopped by the apartment mid-morning to pick up Gina and her suitcase.

"I'm ready for Albuquerque," Gina sang as she skipped from her bedroom.

"Can't wait to spend this week with you. I know we'll have a great time.

We'll find an affordable hotel somewhere near the state fairgrounds. The hotels always give discounts to the exhibitors."

Gina knew this was just what she needed to get over the fact that Pucci had been stolen. And being out of town meant she didn't have to deal with her mother asking her to visit. Her mother did not approve of women driving pickup trucks so wanted Gina to drive when the girls visited. If Joni did drive, then Gina's mother made Joni park around the corner as she did not want her neighbors to see the truck.

Joni easily slid into the routine at the Speech and Theatre Department at the university. The job was mainly typing, collating papers, and using the electric stapler to hold the documents together. Joni had never seen or used an electric stapler and thought it was cute.

At five when she got off work, she stopped at the Dash Inn for a quick hamburger. She wanted food in her stomach before going to The Hut alone to wait for Tom Dixon. If she was going to get drunk, she wanted to get drunk with him.

Joni got to The Hut about six, and it was full of regulars and the frat boys.

"Howdy, Florina," Joni said, trying out her Texas accent like Gina had. "A glass of beer please and two coasters."

"What? No pitcher, not three coasters? Where is Gina?"

"Off at a craft fair in New Mexico. She'll be gone all week so I'm on my own for a few days."

"Well, you won't be lonely if you stop in here. All your buddies are here tonight."

Joni had to repeat the story of Gina going to a craft fair in New Mexico to Pete Groat, then to Boyer and Caffy, then to Joe Ravioli, as well as others who were standing around listening.

"She'll have stories to tell you when she returns," Joni said, hoping that would end the questions.

About an hour later, Tom Dixon walked in the front door and came straight to Joni's side.

"I got here as soon as I could. Couldn't wait to see you." And to Florina, "Would you please get Joni another beer and one for me?" He then turned to face Joni, smiling, and said, "How was your day?"

Joni smiled back. "It was good but I miss Gina. I'm so used to having her around most of the time and having our adventures. I thought about stopping at the record store but that seems like something I need Gina to be here for. She always chooses the new albums we buy."

"I totally understand," Tom Dixon said, sipping his first glass of beer. "I miss Benson, too, but sometimes we just have to get along without our best friends."

Joni burst into song with a few lines from the old camp song about friends being either silver new ones or golden old ones, then paused to take a drink. She looked at Tom Dixon and said, "You wanna be my silver?"

Tom Dixon got it, smiled even wider, and said, "You bet. Maybe even more than that. How about we finish this pitcher and then go over to your apartment? I have a bottle of wine in my car. I'll follow you."

Joni was trying to be coy, but she wanted to take Tom Dixon home as often as she could so wasn't doing too good at the coy part. "Drink up, my troubadour friend! I'm ready to go when you are."

Tom Dixon left a tip for Florina before they left The Hut, took Joni's arm to escort her to the back parking lot, then put her in her truck with a kiss and a promise of more to come when they got back to the apartment.

Once inside the apartment, Joni locked the door. No need to have anyone come inside when Tom Dixon was there. Tom Dixon went into the kitchen with the bottle of wine, saying, "Where's the corkscrew?"

"Top drawer left of the sink."

"Where are the glasses?"

"Wine glass for you in the cabinet over the sink, plastic glass for me. Gina says I'm too much a klutz to drink in her pink Depression glass wineglasses."

Tom Dixon laughed, found the glasses, and poured the wine. "Let's sit on the sofa for a while and talk, Joni."

Oh boy, Joni thought. Talk? What does this mean? Then she said, "Don't forget that the coffee table only has three good legs. Put your drink down carefully or Gina will have my butt."

Tom Dixon settled on the sofa and turned toward Joni. "I really like you, Joni, so you need to know my whole story. You know I am married. I don't wear my wedding ring because I don't want to mark up the neck or fretboard on my guitar, so most people don't know that I am married. And to further complicate things, I have six children."

Joni took a big swig of her wine. She had dealt with married men before, but not one with six children.

"Okay," she said. "What now?"

"I care for you enough that I just wanted you to know. I am not happy in my marriage, my wife is a tyrant, my children don't care about me, but I don't have a way out. I'm a musician, Joni, I play bars for tips and very little cash. If I get divorced, I have no way to pay that much child support. So what do I do? I just stay there and live with it."

"Wow. That certainly is a lot to digest. I'm sure you have thought long and hard about this."

"Yes, I have. I have thought about it, prayed about it, and the only way I can see out of it is to run away and never be found, or just stop living on this earth. Neither one is a very attractive option for me. I enjoy singing, I enjoy entertaining people, and I certainly enjoy you."

Joni sat still for a minute, looking at Tom Dixon and taking a sip of her wine. He waited with anticipation to hear what Joni had to say.

Finally, Joni smiled and said, "Well, Tom Dixon, I'm okay with this if you are. We can just go on as we have been."

Tom Dixon's shoulders finally relaxed. He drank the rest of his glass of wine, took Joni's hand, and pulled her to the bedroom.

"Let's enjoy this while we can."

CHAPTER 34

Friday, March 16. US Army Captain Jim Thompson, the longest-held POW of the Vietnam War, was released after almost nine years of captivity in a Vietcong prison in South Vietnam's Quang Tri province.

· · · · · · · · · · · · · · · · · · · ·

"WELL," JONI SAID TO HERSELF as she left the university Friday afternoon, "a week at this university job and I think I like it. I only wish that Gina were here so I could tell her all about it."

With that, Joni headed for her truck and headed out to The Hut for a Friday afternoon beer, parking behind the bar and entering through the back door.

"*Surprise!*" Gina yelled as Joni came in the door. "Come on over here, I've already poured you a glass of beer from the pitcher."

"Gina, I'm so glad to see you. I wasn't expecting you back so soon."

"The craft fair was so good to Benson that he sold out all of his jewelry before the end of the show, so we decided to come on back to Tempe. We just got back this afternoon and I had him drop me off here. I knew you wouldn't skip a Friday night at The Hut."

The girls both started talking at once, then took turns to tell each other about the past week's adventures. Then Joni stopped and said, "Gina, you got a ring just like Benson's," staring at the huge silver and turquoise ring on Gina's left hand middle finger.

"No, Joni, it isn't a ring just like Benson's. It *is* Benson's!"

"Wow, he gave you his ring? Does that mean you are going steady?"

"Joni, no one 'goes steady' in today's world. We're just really close right now."

"Exclusively?" Joni asked.

"I don't think we are that far along in this relationship yet. We'll see how things turn out as time goes by. Benson is a pretty cool dude and he makes a good living selling his jewelry, both good points in my eyes. I think he and Tom Dixon both know that you and I have been seeing other men since we met them."

"I know that Tom Dixon does. And since he's married, that doesn't give him any right to make a claim on me. But like you and Benson, Tom Dixon and I are very good together when we can get together."

The Hut started to fill up with the regulars, and everyone walked over to welcome Gina back when they saw her.

"Get these girls another pitcher, Florina," Pete Groat yelled after hugging each of the girls. And to the girls, "What's the story, morning glory?"

"Gina just got home from New Mexico and she came to The Hut first. I'm so excited to have her home."

"I'm sure you are," Pete Groat said. "You haven't been here much all week long."

"Things just aren't the same without her," Joni said, smiling at Gina and punching Pete Groat in the arm.

"Hey, what was that for?" Pete Groat exclaimed. Gina burst out laughing.

"Peter Aloysius Groat, you know that Joni isn't strong enough to do any harm to your arm. Just deal with it!" Gina said between her laughs.

"I am, too."

"You are not."

"I am, too."

"You are not." At that point, both girls were laughing so hard they couldn't talk any more.

"Girls, girls, girls," Pete Groat continued, "just enjoy the pitcher of beer I bought you and I'll forget the arm punch."

"Arm punch," Gina said, laughing more. "Is that a new drink? Get it? Punch!"

Pete Groat knew he had been outdone by the girls. He, too, started laughing. "Don't know what I'd do without you Mill Avenue Hussies!"

"I'll drink to that," Gina said, picking up her beer glass and emptying it.

"Me too," Joni chimed in.

The girls finished the pitcher of beer that Pete Groat had bought for them and decided it was time to go back to the apartment. Gina had her suitcase in the storage room of The Hut. The girls stopped there before leaving through the back door to get into Joni's truck.

"It's been quite the week," Gina said as they pulled out of the parking lot.

"Boy howdy," Joni agreed.

CHAPTER 35

Saturday, March 17. A teenager at California's Travis Air Force Base made photographic history as she rushed across the tarmac with her arms wide open to greet her father, a recently freed American prisoner of war. The photograph was taken by Associated Press photographer Slava "Sal" Veder.

. . . .

JONI WAS IN THE KITCHEN heating up water for their morning coffee when Gina came bouncing out of her room.

"I have a great idea, Joni. Let's go to Jerome today and spend the night. We can take your truck and go camping after we explore the mountain and the town."

"What's Jerome?" Joni asked as the teakettle began to whistle. Joni prepared the cups with Kava instant coffee and poured in the water, adding milk and sugar to both.

"Oh, Joni, you are going to love it. It is an old mining town that artists and leftover hippies discovered in the sixties. In the mid-sixties, the town was declared a National Historic Landmark District so no developers can alter the ambience of the town. You're going to love the little shops. We can shop, then go up on the mountain into the woods for the day, then come back to town for our nightcap at the Spirit Room, a really cool bar."

"Wow, sounds like an adventure. Let's have our breakfast and pack up the truck."

Packing was easy. A cooler with a small jug of wine, some pork chops, potato chips, and cheese. A change of clothing to go into town for the evening. Two sleeping bags and some pillows. Toilet paper, of course. Joni rarely went anywhere without spare toilet paper.

"And Space Dog is going with us," Gina said as Joni was stuffing things into a duffle bag. "He loves the mountains."

Joni didn't know how Gina figured out that Space Dog loved the mountains, but it was better not to ask.

After a quick breakfast of oatmeal, the girls loaded everything into the camper shell on the back of Joni's pickup truck. Space Dog jumped into the cab with the girls.

"Woo-hoo," Gina shouted as Joni left the Windbell parking lot. "I *love* adventures."

Joni just smiled. After studying the map, Joni took Broadway all the way across town to the Maricopa Freeway, then got on I-17 heading north. She hadn't been on this road since last year when she came to Tempe for the first time from Salt Lake City where her brother lived. It looked pretty much the same, although by now Joni had come to love the desert. She thought Gina was nuts for living in a place that was flat and looked like Sheetrock, as she recalled thinking at the time. Now it was a place of wonder for her.

The maps told Joni to continue on I-17 until she reached State Highway 279. Joni took the exit and said, "I have to pee."

"Get a grip. There's nothing out here until we get to Cottonwood. Just have to hold it."

"Well, maybe I shouldn't have had that second cup of coffee before we left this morning. Or maybe I should just be like Space Dog, lift my leg and go."

"Joni," Gina said, laughing, "just cross your legs and wait until we get to Cottonwood!"

"Gina, I might remind you that this is a standard shift truck, which means I need to have my left leg for the clutch and my right for the accelerator. Crossing them would make it very difficult to drive."

Now both girls were laughing, which didn't help Joni's bladder situation. Joni stopped at the first gas station she saw. It was a bit run down, but she could deal with it. Back in the truck, Joni kept going to Highway 89A, where she saw a sign to Jerome.

"We made it! We're going to Jerome," she said.

Gina thought Joni was being overly dramatic and said nothing.

The road continued to climb, and soon they could see Jerome up on a hilltop. The road made hairpin turns back and forth.

"I'm not big on heights, Gina."

"Get over it. Jerome is on Cleopatra Hill, just over five thousand feet above sea level. You were with your brother in Utah and that was way higher, so just deal with it."

When they finally got to Jerome, Joni was stunned. So many old houses that were abandoned. "Does anyone live here?" she asked Gina.

"Yes, silly girl. A few hundred. The buildings that are still habitable are people's houses and their businesses. Just find a place to park and we'll go shopping for a bit. It's easy to walk around the town and I want to take you to the place where I bought that James Rome print I have hanging in my bedroom. Maybe he'll be there. That would be so exciting."

Easy to walk around the town? Joni thought, Ha. The whole town is tilted and streets are up and down and curved around.

Joni found a place to park in front of an antique store, and Gina immediately knew the way to the art gallery she had been at more than a year ago when she purchased the James Rome print, before Joni had come to Arizona.

"Welcome, ladies," the proprietor said as Gina and Joni walked through the front door of the art gallery. "What can I do for you today?"

"We were wondering if James Rome was in today. I'd love to meet him," Gina replied.

"Sorry, not today. He's down in Tempe at an art fair in the park. I don't think he'll be back until Monday or Tuesday."

Joni just looked at Gina, thinking, And this was the weekend we chose to come up here?

Gina looked so disappointed. Joni, wanting to make Gina feel better, spoke up. "Well, can we look at some of his work while we're here?"

The proprietor showed the girls to where James Rome's art work was displayed. Gina saw one and ran up to it.

"This one. I have to have this one. It's perfect," she gushed.

It was a pen and ink of Jerome. And within Gina's budget.

After purchasing the print, the girls walked around the town, stopping in at several antique stores and a pottery shop.

"Okay, Joni, it's time to go to the mountain."

"What? We're already on a mountain."

"Look up, Joni, that way," Gina said, pointing. "That's Mingus Mountain and we're going up that way for the afternoon. We'll head on up 89A, the same road we came in on, and stop at the first nice picnic area we see. It's a national forest so it won't be any trouble."

"Okay, but do they have bathrooms in the forest?"

Gina scrunched up her face and shook her head. "No, Joni, but they have lots of trees and you can lean on one and pee when you need to. Remember, you packed toilet paper, which of course you either have to bury or bring back with the trash."

Joni didn't think she would like burying toilet paper, so it would have to go into their trash bag. Or maybe she would drip dry.

The girls walked back to Joni's truck and headed up Highway 89A. It was only about thirty minutes later when Gina yelled, "Turn left here."

Joni did, and soon they were at a nice picnic area that had a picnic table and a barbecue grill.

"Joni, get everything out of the truck and set it on the table. I'll open the wine."

As usual, Joni did what Gina told her to do, and soon the girls were all ready for their picnic. They started with the wine and cheese, and just enjoyed the fresh air of the mountain.

After about an hour, Gina said, "Time to fire up the grill and get those pork chops cooking. We want to be off the mountain before sunset."

As ever, Joni did what Gina told her to do, pouring the charcoal briquettes into the barbecue grill and patting them into an even layer, occasionally grunting "yuk" as her fingers turned black.

"Uh-oh, Gina, we don't have any lighter fluid."

"Not to worry, I brought the newspapers from home. Just crumble them up into balls and put them in the center of the charcoal. It should be enough to get the charcoal briquettes going. And, we'd better have another glass of wine while the briquettes get hot."

The charcoal was ready, the girls put the pork chops on the grill, and Gina put out the paper plates and cutlery on the picnic table.

"Nothing ever tastes as good as food on the mountain," Gina said. "We should do this more often."

Joni agreed that the food tasted better than at home but wasn't sure about more time on a mountain without bathrooms.

After finishing her pork chops and chips, Joni picked up the trash and added it to their trash bag along with the toilet paper, then said, "Gina, it looks like the sun is going down."

"Yup, time to change into our chichi clothing and head on down to the Spirit Room. They usually have live music. And, we can take Space Dog in there with us. He likes a good folk singer."

Joni just shook her head and didn't argue. How did Gina know that Space Dog liked folk music?

Back in Jerome, Joni parked a few blocks from the Spirit Room. As they were walking there, Gina told Joni a bit about it. "It's right around the corner on Main Street, underneath the Connor Hotel."

"Underneath a hotel?" Joni asked. "How does anyone get in there?"

"Joni, Joni, the bar is on street level, the hotel was built above it. And, rumors have it that the hotel is haunted."

"Great, just what we need," Joni said, not really worrying because they planned to sleep in the camper shell on the back of her truck, not in the hotel.

The girls entered the Spirit Room, Space Dog following behind them. The girls sat on stools at the bar. Space Dog lay down between them at their feet under the foot rail.

"What'll it be?" the bartender asked, looking back and forth between Gina and Joni. "And, no pets allowed in here. You'll have to get rid of the dog."

Gina looked at Joni. Joni looked at Space Dog, invisible on the floor, saying, "We don't have a dog in here. We both want a glass of beer."

"Come on, girls, I know you have a dog. I know he's invisible and he's lying on the floor at your feet. You need to get him out of here before I bring your beer."

Joni stood up and motioned for Space Dog to follow her out onto the sidewalk. She came back in and returned to her barstool. The bartender smiled and nodded and went to pour the girls' beer.

"How did he know we had Space Dog?" Joni asked Gina.

"Who knows. Maybe this place really is haunted. Maybe Space Dog has been here before. Maybe the bartender is just full of it, but he was pretty right on about things. Let's hope Space Dog stays outside for a while."

The beer was served, the folk singer started playing, and the girls drank up. Space Dog waited outside for a few minutes, then came back into the Spirit Room and sat down on the floor between Gina and Joni.

Gina motioned for the bartender to refill their glasses. The bartender shook his head. "No dogs allowed. Take him back out and make him stay there."

This time Gina took Space Dog outside. He seemed to listen to her more than he listened to Joni. After a few more beers, it was time to find a place to park the truck overnight and go to sleep. Joni remembered a nice pull-off where they could park the truck that she had seen as they drove into town and headed for that. Fortunately, it was relatively flat, something rare in this mountain town. The girls unrolled their sleeping bags in the back of Joni's truck, pulled out their pillows, and were quickly asleep after a day on the mountain and the beer at the Spirit Room. Space Dog slept between them.

CHAPTER 36

Sunday, March 18. Lieutenant General Tran Van Tra, a Vietcong, believed that the US was shipping munitions from Japan to South Vietnam, a violation of the ceasefire agreement. President Nixon countered that and said that the Communists were sending soldiers and weapons to South Vietnam, also a violation of the ceasefire agreement, and that it was not the US.

• • • • • • • • • • • • • • • • • • • •

THE SOUNDS OF JEROME WAKING up also woke Joni. She reached over and shook Gina, saying, "Time to go home, Gina." Gina pulled her pillow over her head.

"Gina," Joni sang, "remember that James Rome is at the art festival in Tempe. We need to go see him."

That had Gina up and ready to rock and roll. "Okay, let's go. I think we should take 89A over the mountain to Prescott. We can have breakfast there."

Joni quickly secured everything in the camper, and the girls were heading over the mountain to Prescott. The road was only two lanes and had many twists and turns after they passed the picnic area where they had stopped yesterday.

"Uh, Gina," Joni said, "you forgot to mention that this road was so scary."

"Suck it up, Joni. You have a stick shift so you can just downshift into a lower gear on the hills. It's only about an hour from Jerome to Prescott so no big deal."

Right, thought Joni. No big deal when you are sitting in the passenger seat. Still, Joni had to admit that the scenery was spectacular. Soon they passed the city limits sign for Prescott.

"Hey, Joni, pull in right here," Gina yelled, pointing to the parking area on the right. "I had breakfast there once when Leroy B. brought me up here to see his parents' cabin. And Space Dog wouldn't mind getting out either after the trip across the mountain."

"Sounds good to me. I'm sure they have a bathroom in there."

Gina just shook her head and smiled.

After breakfast, the girls picked up Space Dog, took Highway 69 from Prescott over to I-17, and headed south toward Phoenix. In just over two hours, the girls were back at the Windbell and unloaded the truck.

"Okay, Joni, we're going to the Tempe art fair. I want to take the new James Rome print I bought and have him autograph it. The park isn't too far from The Hut so we can stop there afterward for a beer."

"Gina, I just drove home. I don't want to drive anymore."

"Silly girl. We'll use those cute little backpacks your mother made us and we'll walk. You can carry the wine and I'll take the print."

Joni wondered how this was going to work out, her walking that far with a jug of wine in her cloth backpack. The backpacks her mother had made for them had a pattern of Aztec gods in the fabric. But knowing not to argue, she said, "Great, I'll be ready in a minute."

It really wasn't that far to walk from the Windbell to the park where the art fair was being held. Once the girls arrived, they stopped under a tree to have a drink of the wine in Joni's backpack. Then they walked around looking for James Rome. It seemed like half of Tempe was at the fair.

Even Morris the bartender was there. He walked up to the girls and said, "Hello, girls. How you doing today?"

The girls looked at each other, thinking, Morris, the bartender who barely talks to us.

Gina answered. "We're just peachy, thank you very much. Hope you are the same."

Morris smiled and walked on.

"He must be drunk," Gina said. "He never chats with us."

Joni agreed, and the girls walked on.

"Look, Joni, it's James Rome, right over there!" Gina shouted, pulling Joni's arm.

James Rome heard Gina's shout and looked at the girls. He smiled and put out his arm to invite the girls to his booth.

"Hello, I'm James Rome," he said. "And you are?"

"I'm Gina," she said, her dimples showing and tilting her head. "I'm your biggest fan. We were in Jerome yesterday and I bought one of your prints. They told us you would be here today so would you please autograph it?"

"Of course, lovely lady. That's one of my favorite prints of Jerome," he said, pulling out a pen to autograph it.

"And if you'd like a glass of wine, we just happen to have some in Joni's backpack, but you'll have to supply your own glass."

"Not a problem," he answered, reaching behind his counter and pulling up a paper cup. "You never know when or where libations will be found."

The three of them enjoyed the rest of the wine together and chatted, and then the booth became busy.

"Gotta go, girls. Thank you for appreciating my art and I hope to see you in Jerome sometime."

Gina giggled. Joni was surprised. Gina never giggled.

After that, the girls waived goodbye to James Rome and headed to The Hut.

"Phew, Gina, you were starstruck by James Rome."

"Yup. He knocks my socks off. Too bad he's married."

"How do you know that?"

"I asked the art gallery woman when I bought the first print that hangs in my bedroom."

Joni shook her head. "Well, at least now you have Benson."

"Hmmm, I do, don't I?"

The girls went into The Hut, sat at the bar, and ordered a pitcher of beer. The wine had been good, but it wasn't cold like the beer at The Hut.

"So what have you girls been up to?" Florina asked Gina.

"Oh, just hanging out at the art fair. We were in Jerome yesterday and we missed James Rome so we wanted to find him today," Gina said with a wistful look in her eyes.

"Yep, he is something to look at, isn't he?" Florina responded.

The girls looked at Florina with their eyebrows raised. They had never seen Florina interested in a white man before, only Hispanics.

"Uh, yes. He is married, though," Gina said.

"Oh, tough for me," Florina said. "Gotta go, people wanting more beer down the bar. Nice to see you both."

"Gina," Joni said. "We have to walk home. I'm tired and it's late and I have to work tomorrow and be semi-sane at the university. What do you think we should do? Call a taxi?"

Gina looked around the bar and smiled. "No, Joni darling." She pointed her finger at Craig from Colorado who was playing pool, gesturing that he should come over after his shot. He nodded at her, made his shot, missed, and walked over to Gina.

"Oh, Craig darling. We need a ride home. When you finish losing that pool game, can you give us a ride to the Windbell?"

"What makes you think I'm losing?" Craig asked.

"I guess the fact that Boyer just sunk all his balls and then put the eight ball in the pocket will do it," Gina explained.

"Okay, you got me on this one. Buy me a beer and I'll give you a ride home."

The girls bought Craig from Colorado a drink, finished their pitcher, and enjoyed the ride home instead of having to walk.

It was time for another week to begin.

CHAPTER 37

Monday, March 19. The American Indian Movement occupiers of Wounded Knee, South Dakota, released the eleven hostages but continued their standoff and seizure of the Bureau of Indian Affairs building.

....

"I'M STAYING HOME TODAY," GINA said. "I know I just took vacation days with Benson but I have more that I'm going to lose if I don't take them, so I plan to stay in bed all day and read magazines."

"Okay, but you'll be alone. I'm still working at the Speech and Theatre Department at the university."

"Well, at least you are making money to pay the rent. I think there's enough bread and cheese for you to make a sandwich to take with you for lunch if you like."

Joni made her sandwich, said goodbye to Gina, and went off to her temp job.

After work, Joni went straight home because she didn't want to go to The

Hut without Gina. As Joni pulled into the parking lot at the Windbell, she almost hit a parked car when she saw an orange Fiat Spider in the space where Gina always parked near the steps to their building.

Joni quickly parked and ran up the stairs to their second-floor apartment. Flinging the front door open, she yelled, "Gina, did you get Pucci back?"

Gina got out of her bed, laughing. "I thought you might say that! But no, my insurance company found another car just like Pucci and asked if I would want it as my insurance settlement. I said hell yes. Well, maybe I said it in a nicer way, but there is my new car."

"Are you still going to call the car 'Pucci'?"

"Nope. This is Bonanno."

Joni looked at Gina, baffled. "What kind of name is that? Bo-nan-no. Sounds like a banana."

"Joni, Joe Bonanno was only twenty-six when he became the youngest boss of a crime family. He owned a funeral parlor in Brooklyn, which was his way of getting rid of bodies. Maybe he should have owned the Green Ashes Crematorium!"

"So how did you hear about him? I've never heard about him before."

"He lived in Tucson for a while. I think his kid had some sort of ear thing and they put him in a private boarding school in Tucson. They say he moved to Tucson sometime in the sixties."

"So, that's interesting, but why did you choose that name?"

Gina looked at Joni, smiling, and said, "Because he made life what he wanted it to be. Sort of how I live."

Joni agreed. "Well, at least now we can go see your mother again and stop making excuses about why we are not there. She'll never figure out this isn't the same car!"

CHAPTER 38

Friday, March 23. "Killing Me Softly With His Song" by Roberta Flack was number one on the music charts.

· · · · · · · · · · · · · · · · · · · ·

JONI HAD TO WORK OVERTIME today at the university and called Gina just before she got off work. Gina had stayed late at her work, too, since she had taken so many vacation days in a row. "Finally done with collating these tests," Joni said.

"I'll meet you at The Hut. I have *so* much to tell you!"

Joni arrived first since The Hut was only a few blocks from the university, with Gina arriving shortly thereafter. She sat to Joni's left and started talking. "Joni, Joni, guess what happened today?"

"Okay, what?"

"*Max called me and asked me out! Tonight!*

"How did he get your number at work?" Joni asked.

"He said that he saw Joe Ravioli today and Joe Ravioli gave him my number. Remember I gave Joe Ravioli my work number once when he said he would pick me up when I needed a ride, and you were working in another part of town."

Gina had been wanting to go out with Max for a long time, but even when she saw Max at The Hut, he did not appear to be interested in her.

"Wow, Gina, what a score. I know you have been pining for him, even though he paid no attention to you at the Peckerwood party."

"Well, Joni, maybe he was busy that night," Gina said, not wanting to admit that he had not been interested in her that night. "Anyway, he is picking me up tonight at seven to go to dinner, then he'll take me to see *The Poseidon Adventure* and then . . . hopefully doing what I have been wanting to do with him for ages."

"Gina, if he is picking you up tonight, then we had better suck down this beer and head on home so you can get ready."

"So you will be okay all alone?"

"Yup. I have a new song roiling around in my brain and it's time I spent some quality time with my guitar."

The girls drank the pitcher in record time and went home to the Windbell.

Gina dressed in her nicest dress jeans with a filmy blue blouse on top. She added some turquoise jewelry that she had gotten at the craft fair in Albuquerque and put on her turquoise rings, including Benson's. She styled her hair with two dog ears, as the boys always loved that.

Joni cleaned up the living room and shortly thereafter,

THERE CAME A KNOCK AT THE DOOR

Gina was ready by this time, standing and waiting in the living room. "Come on in, sweet thing," she said.

Max walked across the threshold, saying, "Gina, you look lovely tonight. Joni, hello to you, too."

"Anyone want a drink?" Joni asked. Both Max and Gina shook their heads.

After Max and Gina left the apartment, Joni pulled out her Gibson LG-1 and sat on the sofa, quietly strumming in the key of C. That was her best vocal range, or sometimes A, depending upon the tune she came up with.

My friends all tell me I should write a love song
All they see's the sparkle in my eyes
They don't know the spark is only moonlight
on my teardrops
That fall to wash away your foolish lies

Joni had been drinking wine, convinced it made her write better songs, and passed out in her bed right after working on the new song. She never heard Gina and Max come back to the apartment.

CHAPTER 39

Saturday, March 24. The 591st and final episode of the *Lassie* TV series was aired in syndication. "Love Train" by The O'Jays was number one on the music charts.

. . . .

JONI AWOKE FIRST AND PUT the water on to boil for their instant Kava coffee. Then she walked to the apartment office to pick up a newspaper so she could check for any new job openings that she might like. When she got back to the apartment, she gently shook Gina's bed and said, "Coffee's up and you're not!"

Ordinarily, Gina would snip at Joni and pull the covers over her head. This morning was different. Gina was smiling!

"Oh, Joni, this was the best date I have ever had. When we got back here, Max pulled me to my bed and it was marvelous. When he left, he said, 'This is the most beautiful way to end my days.'"

Joni thought, "My days?" Maybe Gina heard it wrong.

"Did he ask you out again?" Joni asked.

"No, but I'm sure he'll want to come back. Get it? *Come* back."

"Quit the nostalgia, let's have breakfast and get ready for the day."

After breakfast and checking the want ads, finding nothing that was better than her temp job at the university, Joni said, "Hey, Gina, what do you want to do today?"

"Come on, Joni, let's go to The Hut. Maybe Max will be there today. I'd love a repeat! You drive your truck and I'll take Bonanno in case I get to go to Max's house. And there is a pool tournament at The Hut today and there should be lots of guys there since it is the weekend."

The Hut was quiet when they arrived. The TV was not turned on, no rowdy jokes, nothing, not even the jukebox. There was no pool tournament in progress. Florina was behind the bar, and she was not smiling. Gina and Joni walked to two empty stools at the bar and sat down.

"A pitcher of beer and two glasses, *por favor*," Gina said as usual, smiling and tilting her head.

Florina walked up to the girls, without a pitcher of beer, glasses, or coasters, and looked at each of them.

"You don't know?" she questioned.

"Know what?" Gina said, making her rat face because she really wanted a beer.

"Max," Florina answered. "Max..." and then she started crying.

"Max?" Gina said. "I was out with him last night and we had a wonderful time."

"When did you see him last?" Florina asked, suddenly serious.

"Just after two last night when he kissed me good-bye in our living room and then left to go back to his apartment."

"Gina, you were the last person to see him alive."

Gina shook her head over and over until Joni thought Gina might fall off the barstool.

Florina continued. "Max killed himself last night."

Joni snapped and put the pieces together. "Gina," she said, "remember that you told me the last thing Max said to you was that his date with you was the most wonderful way to end his days, *not* his 'day' but his 'days.' Oh, Gina, I am so sorry."

The girls were all crying by this point. Joe Ravioli and Boston Jack had been listening to the exchange and came up to hug Gina with condolences.

"Give me a shot of tequila, Florina," Gina said. "I need it."

"Put it on my tab," Joe Ravioli said. "And one for Joni, too."

When Florina brought the shots of tequila, Joni looked at her and said, "Anyone know why? Max always seemed so down to earth and shy, not depressed or anything."

Florina closed her eyes and took a deep breath. "You know, Joni, we all thought Max liked guys more than girls, but no one said anything about it. It's not easy nowadays to be that way, so most people just keep it hidden. Maybe his date with Gina was him trying to prove he could like girls. Or who knows. Max never talked much and was always polite. Never caused any trouble here."

Gina heard what Florina said and started crying even more. "Joni, please take me home. Florina, can I leave my car here overnight? The top is up in case it rains."

"Gina, we will take care of you however we need to."

Joe Ravioli spoke up. "Gina, I'll watch out for your car. I don't live too far from here."

Joni took Gina home in her truck. She helped her up the stairs. "Do you want to eat something?"

"No. I want to go to bed. Why did he do that? Is something wrong with me?"

"Gina, nothing is wrong with you. People who don't want to live are the ones who need help. Max just wanted to have fun on his way out. And you provided that. He had fun. He just had had enough of living, whatever his problem was. If he liked boys instead of girls, well, that just isn't tolerated much in today's world."

"I'm certainly glad this is a weekend and I don't have to work. I plan to spend the entire day today and tomorrow in bed. *You* are going to do the cooking and all I want is soup. How bad can you mess up opening a can of soup and pouring it into a pan? This whole thing with Max *sucks* and you know how I feel about things that suck. Or maybe sometimes sucking is okay," Gina said, looking like her old self.

With that ending, Joni knew that after a weekend of rest, Gina would be okay.

CHAPTER 40

Sunday, March 25. Despite the Paris Peace Accords having been signed less than two months earlier, the North Vietnamese Army began the Battle of Tong Le Chon against the Ninety-Second Ranger Battalion of South Vietnam, a siege of the Tonle Cham Camp in South Vietnam's Binh Phuoc province.

. . . .

GINA AWOKE FIRST, HAVING SPENT most of Saturday in her bed. She filled the singing teapot and set it on the stove to boil. While it was heating, Gina filled two coffee cups with instant Kava coffee. She allowed the teapot to boil and whistle until Joni finally got out of bed. Gina laughed to herself and poured the water into the coffee cups, still stirring in the sugar and milk as Joni walked into the kitchen.

"*What do you want?*" Joni shouted.

Smiling and showing her dimples, Gina said, "I am much better today. I want a hamburger but I don't want to go to the Dash Inn or The Hut. I really don't want to see people we know today. Let's have our coffee, watch the Sunday morning news, which I know you like, and then head out to Minder Binders for a burger and some beer. Time to get back into the world, even though the world is a lot smaller with the loss of Max." She shook her head.

"Okay, okay. Let's just go have a great meal downstairs at Minder Binders, play some pool upstairs, and have a nice adventure."

The girls carried their coffee to the living room, and Joni turned on the RCA Trans Vista color television and sat down beside Gina on the sofa to watch the morning news.

"Not much happening today," Joni said. "Like who cares if the American family size is shrinking and the US might be heading toward zero population growth? I am thankful for birth control, especially since I live in Tempe with so many single men."

"Joni, you are always thinking about men. Didn't you pay attention to the article about the POWs still being held in Laos?"

"I paid attention, but not too much because it made me think about Pilot and I don't want to go there again. He served in Vietnam, and other than teaching him to fly a plane under the radar so he could maybe run drugs, what did that get him?"

"Joni, you aren't focusing. Pilot was probably just a dumb drug dealer. You need to let it go, just like I need to let Max go in my heart and mind."

Joni looked directly at Gina. Gina was not usually that direct and didn't talk about her emotions. Joni knew that Gina meant business.

"Okay, you are right. No more talk about Pilot. Let's talk about what we are going to wear today to Minder Binders."

"Joni, you always wear the same thing. And since we won't know most of the people there, you can wear whatever you want and no one will know it looks like all of your other clothing. I personally am going to wear a shirt that looks good when I lean over the pool table so I can hustle us some beer."

As the opening time for Minder Binders approached, the girls went to their bedrooms and started getting ready. Joni once again chose her dark brown shirt her mother had made her that matched her bronze earrings, a shirt she wore often, and a ring she had gotten in Austin years ago that matched the earrings. Since they didn't expect to see anyone they knew, Joni thought that her choice was just fine. Gina chose a low-cut black tank top over which she put on her "H" apron, which she called her "heroin apron." The antique white apron had an *H* embroidered on it. Gina liked to wear only the "H" apron with nothing under it, but decided that probably wasn't appropriate for Minder Binders so put a tank top on first.

"You'd better drive, Joni. I'm up for a lot of beer today. And look, Space Dog wants to go with us."

Joni looked to the same place Gina was looking and agreed. "Yup, he wants to go to Minder Binders. I think he loves the peanut shells on the floor."

The girls left the apartment, locked the door, and walked down to Joni's truck. Space Dog jumped into the front seat with them. Joni quickly took them to McClintock and University where the big red barn that was Minder Binders was located. Joni pulled into the back parking lot. Gina opened her door long enough for Space Dog to jump out.

The girls walked in the back door, and Gina chose a booth for them to sit at. Joni stopped at the ladies' room, Gina just shaking her head since the apartment was not too far from the bar.

When Joni joined Gina at the booth, she said, "What are you having today?"

"A hamburger and a good man would do it for me!"

Joni laughed. But inside she was very happy because it meant Gina was starting to be okay about Max.

"I'll join you in both, plus let's have some beer."

The girls ordered and sipped on their beer while waiting for their hamburgers.

"This is just what you wanted, Gina. I'm not seeing anyone we know."

Gina smiled. Once again, Joni was so glad that Gina was going to be okay. Then Gina's eyes opened wide and she started shaking her head slowly.

"What?" Joni said. "What do you see?"

Gina smiled. "Turn around and you'll see, too."

There were Benson and Tom Dixon coming in the front door of Minder Binders. They saw the girls and walked directly to their table.

"Well, hello you sweet thing," Benson said to Gina. "And you, too, Joni."

Gina just beamed. Joni said, "What are you two doing in a place like this?" and then laughed.

Benson responded while slipping into the booth beside Gina. "Tom Dixon had a day off today and we both wanted to see our girls." Joni was thinking, "Our girls?"

"You weren't at your apartment or The Hut or any of the bars on Mill Avenue, so we came up here thinking maybe we'd find you. Thankfully we found you because I wasn't looking forward to checking out all the other bars in Tempe."

"How did you know we might be in a bar?" Gina said to the boys, turning her head to the side and sticking her fingers in her dimples.

"Oh, just a hunch," Tom Dixon answered, shaking his head. Everyone at the table was laughing. Tom Dixon slid into the booth beside Joni.

Tom Dixon and Benson ordered burgers and beer and asked the waitress to bring them at the same time that she brought the girls' orders.

The burgers arrived quickly, and the conversation stopped as everyone enjoyed their lunch.

"So what are you girls up to today?" Benson finally asked after putting his burger down.

"We're up for anything that's up," Gina said, looking directly at Benson, who started laughing again.

"You are so predictable, Gina," he said. "Actually I was looking for you. I have a weeklong craft fair at a market in New Mexico and I thought if you have some vacation days left, you might want to go with me. We had such a good time when you went with me to Albuquerque before."

Gina's eyes were wide open. "Vacation time, you bet. I'll find some. When are you leaving?"

"Tomorrow. Can you be ready by then?"

"Honey, I'm ready now!"

Joni and Tom Dixon were watching the exchange. Joni knew that Gina was going to find a way to get out of work for a week.

Tom Dixon turned to Joni and said, "I thought we might be able to come over to your apartment this afternoon. If you didn't have any other plans."

Joni shrugged, then smiled and said, "*You* are my plans today!"

"But Gina," Benson said, "will you be able to fit in my visit and still be ready to leave in the morning."

"Benson, I'd fit you in anywhere!" Everyone was laughing. Gina continued. "Joni drove us here and I'm going to ride back with her. You know where we live so we'll see you there."

Benson was surprised because he had driven and expected Gina to ride back to the apartment with him, and Tom Dixon with Joni, but the same as everyone, he knew better than to argue with Gina. He didn't think he had ever seen anyone argue with Gina.

Once in Joni's truck, Joni asked, "So why didn't you ride with Benson?"

They had just gotten out onto McClintock and were crossing the arroyo. Minder Binders was surrounded by farmland.

"Pull over," Gina said to Joni. "Right here."

Joni did what Gina directed and pulled over to the right side of the road. Gina opened her door. Space Dog leaped out.

"What just happened?" Joni asked.

"He got out, Joni. He got out and he isn't coming back," Gina said as Space Dog ran through the arroyo and into the fields. "He isn't ours anymore."

Joni wanted to cry but knew better. Plus, she didn't want to smear her mascara since Tom Dixon was coming to the apartment.

"Okay, I'll deal with it. Sure was a fun time while we had him."

"Isn't that how most of life is? A fun time while we had them?"

Joni didn't say anything, just shook her head and pulled back onto McClintock and headed for the apartment.

The boys pulled into the Windbell parking lot shortly after Gina and Joni arrived and headed upstairs to the apartment.

"I can't stay too long," Benson said to Tom Dixon. "I have a lot of things to get ready to leave tomorrow."

"I figured that," Tom Dixon replied. "Just give me enough time for a quick bout with Joni and then we can leave."

"I'll just help Gina get ready. I'll have her to myself for the whole week."

The girls had left the front door to the apartment open as the weather was quite pleasant. The boys entered and saw Joni in the kitchen starting to make the girls' famous ice cream grasshoppers. Gina was in her room sorting through her clothing. Benson joined

Gina in the bedroom, and Tom Dixon joined Joni in the kitchen.

"Hello, you gorgeous thing," he said. Joni blushed. "You know we can't stay long because Benson needs to get ready for the craft fair tonight. But maybe we'll be able to stay just long enough."

Joni smiled and quickly put the ice cream back in the freezer.

"These grasshoppers can wait. Let me show you to my room!"

The boys left about an hour later. Joni took Gina's dirty clothing down to the laundry in their apartment building, then helped her get ready to leave the next day. Joni was starting to get used to Gina not being home.

CHAPTER 41

Monday, March 26. The government of South Vietnam released one of its most well-known political prisoners, former presidential candidate Truong Dinh Dzu, who had been incarcerated for more than five years after running in the 1967 presidential election on a platform of negotiating for peace with the Communist Vietcong. Women were admitted into the London Stock Exchange for the first time.

• •

GINA HAD GONE WITH BENSON, and Joni was on her own for at least a week. She had the job at the university, which was close to The Hut, should she want to go, plus she was eager to get back to singing and writing some songs. She had never really lived alone, but maybe this was going to turn out okay for a while.

CHAPTER 42

Thursday, March 29. Two months after the signing of the Vietnam peace agreement, the last US combat troops leave South Vietnam as Hanoi frees many of the remaining American prisoners of war held in North Vietnam. America's direct eight-year intervention in the Vietnam War was at an end. In Saigon, some seven thousand US Department of Defense civilian employees remained behind to aid South Vietnam in conducting what looked to be a fierce and ongoing war with Communist North Vietnam.

. . . .

GINA WAS STILL IN NEW Mexico at the craft fair with Benson. Joni's temp agency didn't have any work for her that day, but she wasn't worried. The job at the university hadn't ended, but the Speech and Theatre Department didn't need her today. She had the next month's rent stashed away in her closet. Joni was ready for a day to herself. Maybe the April *Cosmopolitan* was on the newsstands and she could pick that up to read before Gina got home.

After a quick breakfast of toast and cheese, Joni picked up her notebook to catch up on her journal. There was so much to chronicle. Then

THERE CAME A KNOCK AT THE DOOR

Since Joni was alone in the apartment, she decided to walk to the door to see who it was rather than just yell and tell the person who was knocking to enter. Joni opened the door and saw Wheeler.

"Hi there, trucker boy. I haven't seen you in a long time. Come on in!"

Wheeler stepped into the living room and closed the door. He wasn't smiling or his usual self when he saw Joni.

"Joni, we have to talk."

Uh-oh, Joni thought. Don't they all start this way when it's over? Well, not all of them, she reflected. Most of them just go away and don't even say anything.

Not wanting to be rude, Joni said, "Coffee or beer, mimosa or me?" She couldn't help throwing herself into the mix.

"A beer if you have one." Joni got Wheeler a beer, and they both sat down on the sofa.

"It's been a rough few weeks for me, Joni."

Joni was thinking, For *you*? You should have been around here.

Wheeler continued. "I jackknifed my truck down close to Tucson on I-10 and—"

"Wait, jackknifed?"

"Oh, I forget sometimes when I talk trucker language that you wouldn't understand. A jackknifed truck is where the trailer and the cab get at an angle so they resemble the acute angle of a folding pocketknife. When that happens, you can't drive the truck and it stays where it is until a tow truck arrives. And because it was on the interstate, blocking traffic, several police cars came to assist."

"Wow, bummer," Joni said, shaking her head.

"It only gets worse. I had picked up a load in El Paso to deliver to Phoenix. The trailer was locked when I picked it up, and I had to sign a paper with the shipper stating that no one was to unlock the trailer doors until I arrived in Phoenix. Well, the police weren't having any of that and cut the lock off. Inside the trailer were a lot of tomato plants that I was delivering to the nursery in Phoenix. But I didn't know that at least a third of the plants were marijuana plants. The police took me to the station and detained me until they reviewed all the paperwork that proved I had nothing to do with what was in the trailer. They let me go but kept the truck."

"Did Phil Fancy have anything to do with this?" Joni asked.

"I may never know. I called him and quit right after I got out of the Tucson police station. And Joni, I have to tell you something."

Great, Joni thought. This is almost like "We have to talk."

"I'm engaged to be married, Joni. I didn't tell you before because I haven't seen her in over a year,"

Wheeler revealed, looking down at his feet. "Maybe I was having doubts, but now I just don't know."

Joni steeled herself against crying and said, "So what now, Wheeler? Are you going to drive for another trucking company? Are you going back to your fiancé?"

"I'm gonna stay off the road for a while, Joni, and I don't know what I am going to do about my fiancé," Wheeler said. "I'll go and spend some time with my Indian friends on the Gila reservation. See where I should go next. Mend my bones and heal my mind. I may go up to Arcosanti and help my friends there doing the construction. Arcosanti is going to be a marvelous place. It's an experiment in living frugally with a limited environmental footprint, a new concept." He took her hand in his and kissed her palm. "Today I'm not saying goodbye, only catch you on the flip-flop if I don't go back to my fiancé and if you are still interested."

Joni knew better than to ask much about the future, especially from a man, even more from one who was engaged to be married. First looking down, and then up into his eyes, breathing deeply, she said, "Do you think you'll ever settle down? Stay in one place?" thinking, Stay with me?

"You never know, Joni, you never know."

CHAPTER 43

Friday, March 30. Ellsworth Bunker resigns as US ambassador to South Vietnam. There was no further news coverage of the Vietnam War that day.

. . . .

JONI TOLD HER TEMP AGENCY that she was not able to work today. She just wasn't up to it. The temp agency told her that she could go back to the Speech and Theatre Department on Monday as they had asked for her to come back. Gina was still away with Benson; Wheeler had basically told her it was over. She needed time to herself and her guitar. When the morning news was over, Joni turned off the television and took her guitar out of its case. Poured herself a glass of wine. Sat down on the sofa with her paper and pen, jotted down a few lines and then started singing.

Our hours together were not very many
But you'll be with me in my heart for a while
Sweet loving passes with the blink of an eye
Sweet memories always bring me a smile

That afternoon Joni decided to take a nap. After a few hours asleep, she was awakened by the front door opening. Even though the girls did not lock their door very often, Joni thought it was prudent to lock it when she was alone, so she was surprised when the door clicked open.

"Lucy, I'm home!" Gina yelled. Joni jumped out of bed and ran into the living room.

Benson had dropped Gina off at the Windbell and then, after kissing her goodbye, left to return to his own apartment with a "See you soon" and a big smile.

"Pour me a big one, Joni, I have so much to tell you!" Gina spent the rest of Friday afternoon telling Joni stories of her adventures with Benson.

"I think we should stay in tonight and get ready for whatever is going to happen next. How about a shot of brandy in a cup of coffee before we go to sleep?" Gina phrased that as a question, but Joni knew it was an order. Not that Joni minded having a shot of brandy before bed. She scurried off to the kitchen to heat up the water to make their instant Kava coffee, then added a hefty shot of brandy to the coffee cups.

Joni served the coffee at the gateleg table, and both girls sat down.

"Joni, I think I'm going to quit my job and start working the craft fairs with Benson. I love jewelry and especially turquoise and, and..."

"And what, Gina?"

"And I think I'm falling in love with Benson. We make a good team and I want to be with him for a while. I could do the craft fairs with him and then do temp work like you do in between."

"I don't know, Gina. Do you think you are okay with not having that cushy paycheck you get every two weeks?" Joni was concerned for her friend.

"Yup. At least I'm going to give it a try. And if it doesn't work out, well, I'll just move back here and live with you."

"Oh, Gina, I'd always welcome you home wherever I am. I think I should be able to keep this two-bedroom apartment now that my temp agency has upped my salary and they seem to be keeping me employed, especially at the university. I'm okay with whatever you want to do."

"Joni, I'll send you money for my share of the rent because I want to keep my things here. You can handle the electricity, right? I'm not ready to move in with Benson just yet. Just travel with him for a while and see what happens."

"That's a great deal, Gina. Of course I can take care of the electricity myself. I'll miss you, but there will always be adventures."

Then Joni stopped talking and lowered her eyes.

"*What?*" Gina bellowed. She knew something was up.

"I guess I'd better tell you what is going on," Joni said to Gina. "Wheeler was here visiting while you were traveling with Benson and said that he plans to stop driving a truck. He also told me he has been engaged to be married but he wasn't sure what he wanted to do about that. He said he was going to spend time with his friends on the Indian reservation and then go to Arcosanti to help them build a city. I don't know if I will ever see him again." She was trying not to cry.

"Arcosanti? Where in the world is that?"

"Wheeler said it is up north about an hour from Phoenix. The idea came from Paolo Soleri. He started the project a few years ago to demonstrate how urban conditions could be improved while not harming the Earth. Wheeler said he is always looking for volunteers."

"And stop that crying, Joni. It's not like this is a first for you."

The girls were quiet for a bit, and Gina went to refill the brandy in their coffee cups. Mostly brandy, not a lot of coffee. As she walked back to the living room with the coffee cups, Gina said, "Well, Joni, you've done it again."

"What are you talking about?" Joni said, taking her coffee cup from Gina.

"First a pilot. Now a trucker. Both of the affairs ended and left you alone. You certainly have a way with boyfriends."

"Well, I guess I'm over it then. No more boyfriends in the transportation business," Joni said. "Someone who flies, someone who drives. That about exhausts it."

Gina just smiled, showing her dimples, tilting her head to the right and looking straight at Joni.

"Oh really? What about that riverboat captain you met at the Melody Lounge?"

EPILOGUE

GINA SPENT TWO YEARS TRAVELING to craft fairs with Benson. The pair made a great sales team and they netted enough money to open a jewelry business together in Scottsdale, an upscale community adjacent to Tempe and Phoenix. Joni's job at the university became a permanent job and she enjoyed having her workplace so close to The Hut, where she could continue to see her friends. Wheeler spent eight months on the Indian reservation and then moved to Arcosanti to help Paolo Soleri build it. One weekend, he came back to Tempe and asked Joni to marry him. She agreed.

Tom Dixon finally had enough with the situation with his wife and six children, and one day bought a gun and blew his head off.

ABOUT THE AUTHOR

BARBARA LIGHT LACY'S parents were ahead of their time, teaching her "Be whatever you want to be; do whatever you want to do. Just be home by curfew!"

That probably explains why this free spirit, musician, singer/songwriter, novelist and poet, writes books that run from cookbooks to novels.